The Frighteners

The underworld of a big midland city is badly frightened. Tough as its members are, they are not tough enough to stand up to the agents of the big boys from 'the Smoke', who are seeking to extend their field of operations—especially when those agents employ against them a silent, deadly weapon which can reduce a man's hand to nothing or leave his body one vast burn.

The police are keenly aware of the new and dangerous threat posed by the London gang. Under the leadership of the Assistant Chief Constable, co-ordination is established between the city and regional crime squads, which include several police characters who figured in Roger Busby's widely acclaimed previous novel, *Robbery Blue*. Bit by bit the police piece together the evidence and identify the secret weapon, but they lack the cogent proof that would stand up in court. The working together of the different branches of the police force, their rivalries, jealousies and ultimate dedication are as graphically portrayed as are the tactics of the local underworld, for once on the same side as the police.

As the ding-dong struggle rages, Roger Busby builds up suspense with a sure hand. The unexpected and ironical means by which the London gang are finally brought to a rough justice reveal his realistic appraisal both of underworld organization and of the methods by which the police are occasionally forced to proceed.

by the same author

ROBBERY BLUE

The Frighteners

Roger Busby

The Crime Club
Collins, 14 St James's Place, London

ISBN 0 00 231235 2

© Roger Busby, 1970

Printed in Great Britain
Collins Clear-Type Press
London and Glasgow

For Mo.

CHAPTER I

THE CUE BALL scattered the triangle of reds and curved back on to the cush. Miller played a straight shot across the table and the blue cracked into a side pocket. The harsh pool of bright light which flooded down on to the green baize played on the moist forehead of the billiard hall owner standing at the foot of the table, clasping and unclasping his hands in a nervous gesture.

'Please, Mr Miller, just this week, business hasn't been so good and I ain't made more than a few quid. Can't we leave it over till the next time?'

A red and then the pink. Miller leaned over the table, balancing the cue in his hands.

'I told you before, you can't have insurance without paying the premiums, dad. My boss is a businessman too, and you don't think I'd be wasting my time in a dump like this unless he was worried about you, do you? So cut the hard times chat and cough up, I've heard it all before.'

Another red dropped and Miller slammed the black away, the seven ball smacking the leather rim before dropping into the stringed pouch.

'But what am I to pay with if I don't have the cash? Just this once Mr Miller, please.'

Miller stood motionless over the table and breathed a heavy sigh. 'I can't do it in your own interests, dad. You're paying for a service and if you stop, then the service ends and you know what that means . . .' He nodded across the table, to where a big man in a bulging pin-striped suit detached himself from the shadows, smiling.

'You know Eddie, dad. Don't want to upset him, do you?'

The owner looked around him, licking his lips. He had bought the billiard hall from a bankrupt six months ago and had put up a big red neon sign outside spelling Billiards, and a flashing arrow to attract the customers. It had done that and he'd told the callers who said they were insurance men offering their special policy cover that he was doing all right and would look after his own property. The next night the sign went out, smashed by several house bricks. When the men came again he agreed to pay. He tried to stop his hands shaking. The hall was almost empty, a couple of youngsters with no home to go to playing snooker at the far end and his helper putting the dust covers on the other tables.

'I can't pay, not this week,' and his voice broke. 'Look, I'll make it up next week, I promise, every penny . . .'

Miller cracked his cue down on the table, snapping it in half, turned and raised the splintered stump. His face was livid with anger and the neck veins pulsed hard against his shirt collar. In contrast to the sudden flash of violence, his voice was soft and gentle.

'Don't make me mad, dad, just get the money or else there's going to be accidents.' He nodded almost lazily across the table and the big man raised his elbow and struck the light meter a sudden blow. The front of the machine shattered and leaned drunkenly from the wall mounting. Miller dropped the piece of the cue and walked along the table.

'I'm getting tired of you, dad. Perhaps I'll have to go

and get the rest of the boys and make a good job of it, eh Eddie?'

He couldn't stop the trembling which had spread to every part of his body. Any more damage and he would be out of business. At the first sign of trouble, the two young players had left their game and slipped away leaving the peeling glass panelled exit door swinging. A pile of dust covers lay draped across the table. The helper had vanished too. He looked at the cracked paint on the walls, the pitted lino, tasted the cigarette smoke which still hung in the air. Was it worth it? If he didn't pay the protection money, it would be his family next, his little daughter coming home from school with her face laid open by a razor. He shuddered at the sudden compelling image, and his voice was a strangled sob as he turned to the office in a partitioned corner of the drab room.

Miller counted the notes, £50 in fives and ones.

'There we are, nothing to get excited about. You'll be all right as long as you do as you're told, remember that.' He gestured to Eddie who was leaning against the wall and they walked to the door. 'Same time next week, dad. Be good.'

Miller pushed the wad of notes into an inside pocket and smoothed his suit as they stepped out on to the pavement. Eddie dogged his footsteps, breathing in the crisp air. Miller sniffed the night, the wet deserted pavements and the special odours of a big city back street.

'I thought the old sod was going to give us a bit of bother there, mate. I thought we was going to have to give him a bit of boot to teach him a lesson.'

They turned the corner into an alley where their black Zephyr was parked without lights. Eddie moved to the passenger door.

'Where we going now, then?'

'The all-night café on the ring road. He's got debts too.'

Miller fumbled for his keys in the darkness and did not see the figures until they were beside him. 'What the 'ell . . .' Miller was startled.

The man was gripping his arm. It was a tight grip and the fingers dug in, hurting. 'Eh . . . what's going on?'

The voice which came out of the dark was cold and flat. 'Easy, mate. We just want a chat. Let's keep it friendly, eh?'

'You the law?' Miller was rattled. Fancy getting jumped in the dark with the cash on him. He panicked. 'Quick, Eddie . . . clobber 'em.'

There was a groan across the car and he saw Eddie fall over the bonnet. Behind him were two more shapes.

'What's the game . . .'

No answer. The man gripping his arm forced him towards the back of the car. The door was open. 'Get in,' he commanded, pushing him into the rear seat.

Miller watched them drag Eddie to the other door and drop his slumped body on to the floor space between the seats. 'He's out,' said another voice. The doors closed and he could see three men in the car. The one in the driving seat leaned over, 'Keys,' he demanded, and before Miller could protest, he plucked the car keys from his hand.

The car moved out of the alley and in the light from the passing street-lamps Miller took a careful look at his captors. The man beside him had his feet on Eddie's slumped form. Miller could see the dim outline of an iron bar in his hand. His head was singing and he was having difficulty marshalling his thoughts. These geezers ain't the law, not with iron bars they're not, and if they're not the law . . . He found it impossible to finish the sentence. The man in the front was instructing the driver.

'Where you taking me?' Miller managed at last.

'Shut up or you'll get the same as your mate,' came the answer. No one else spoke.

The car threaded through the side-streets. The bloke from the café and some of his cronies, thought Miller; turned nasty; well, if that was it, they'd get theirs, they'll be bloody sorry when Farrow hears about it. He'll know what to do, but in the meantime, it's my skin.

'You won't get away with this. I got you marked and we'll get you. When the lads get to hear . . .'

The man in the front seat cut him short. 'If he opens his mouth again, give him a tap.'

The one beside him prodded him with the iron bar. Miller was badly frightened now.

They drove in silence across the city and out along the Eastway fly-over, past the railway sidings and into a driveway near a deserted goods yard. Miller recognized the area. It was a slum clearance district, given over to waste land and scrapyards until the building programme began.

The big car lurched through the open double gates of a scrap-metal yard and followed the narrow track between the high piles of junk. Derelict cars stacked on top of one another cast hideous shadows in the faint glow of the orange mercury-vapour lamps from the distant fly-over. The car stopped in a clear space near the centre of the scrapyard and Miller was pushed roughly out of the back door. The headlights etched the mountains of broken metal and hurt Miller's eyes as he was dragged into the twin beams. He could smell the animal stench of his own fear as the adrenalin coursed through his veins. The men were in the darkness standing around him, silent, just black menacing figures. Miller screwed up his eyes in the harsh light from the car. They stayed in the shadows so that he could not see them; even the man gripping his arm was just a shape.

There was a movement outside the light and Miller saw the unconscious Eddie, bundled like a big lumpy sack from the car and then dragged into the headlight beams. The big man lay spreadeagled on the uneven ground, the hair at the back of his head matted with the dull oozing blood from his wound.

'OK,' said the flat voice, 'get the gear out.'

The figures moved away and Miller could feel his arms pinned more tightly now as the man who was doing the talking came over to him.

'I know all about you, Miller, and I know all about your racket. Now we're going to give you a little lesson tonight, sort of a message to take back to your boss, because from now on your operation's over . . .'

Miller's voice was cracked. 'Look, mates, you got it wrong. Me and Eddie, we're just the minders, it's no good working us over. We don't mean nothing . . .' He felt a sharp prod in his kidneys.

'Shut up, Miller. Like I said, it's nothing personal.'

Miller had been distracted briefly by the voice, now he saw the spluttering white flame which suddenly entered his field of vision. He was paralysed with terror and his head felt as if it would burst. The fingers bit into his arms. The burning torch came closer, moving near to the ground, shrouded in a pin-wheel of white hot sparks. He could make out a man, his face hidden by a welding mask behind the light which glowed at the end of a long rod. There should be a roaring sound, his brain insisted, but instead there was absolute silence, just the white-hot flame.

'All right, get it over with,' commanded the voice. 'You remember this, Miller, and if the law finds out what happened tonight, you're next.'

The man in the mask was standing over the prostrate figure on the ground. The end of the rod glowed with eyeball-searing intensity as it swung in a tight arc and Miller watched, transfixed with horror, as Eddie's outstretched hand disintegrated in the white heat. His head was swimming and he could feel an awful vertigo sweeping over him. Oh God, they've burned off his hand. They've burned Eddie's hand. The light turned red as the blood racing through his body veiled his eyes. Through the pounding inside his head, he could just hear the voice, speaking almost kindly now. 'Take your friend home, Miller, and remember, no law, no hospital, no doctors, or you're next. Just let your boss know we'll be in touch.' The hands released him and he fell forward retching uncontrollably as the sweet smell of burnt flesh overpowered him.

CHAPTER II

CITY TREES are never the same. Bred in captivity, they hang limply, coated grey from the ever-present dust suspended in an inverted cone over the industrial complex. They march in dejected discipline down the central reservation of the dual carriageway, sharing the narrow strip of grass with the soulless telegraph poles and the concrete lamp standards, painted garish green in contrast to the drab foliage. The spring was a constant surprise to the city, he thought, as the trees and roadsigns slipped past the car windscreen. Summer was easier to handle, just a heavy humid heat, cloyed with the million smells of a cramped community, but the spring, the first breath of life since the frozen grip of winter was relaxed, that was something else. The city looked at the spring, turned it over, examined its light breezes, but it was old and tired, he thought, and because it hated change, it ignored the spring and waited for this countryside trespasser to go away. It was different where he came from in the country. There the spring was a welcome visitor, an apéritif to summer, a thing to be watched blooming over the fields and hedges and the towns and villages too small as yet, to have been influenced by their big concrete and tarmaced brother.

He sighed to himself and shifted his grip on the steering-wheel. The spring was something to be enjoyed, but the city had no time for pleasures beyond the flashing neon of the night-clubs, the cinemas, bingo halls and bowling alleys. Townsfolk were too busy in their office blocks or throbbing grimy factories to spare a thought for the springtime, except perhaps a brief week-end excursion in a traffic jam. He turned left off the ring road, with a nod of compassion to the trees, even more stunted now as the city centre approached.

The road cut through a new Corporation housing estate of flats and maisonettes, already sooty from the ever-corrosive atmosphere. They dropped below as his car followed the fly-over, a long black arch with the multi-story complex of the city centre rearing above it. The car dropped down again, round a traffic island, passing under another leg of the fly-over, between the giant stilts on which the road was perched. He swung into a driveway, backed between the white-painted slots of the parking space, and switched off the engine. He stretched, gripping the steering-wheel and flexing his neck muscles, then looked at his wristwatch. It was 9.15 a.m. on a bright April morning. He left the car and crossed the parking area to a varnished door set in the oatmeal brickwork of the building. As he stepped through the door, he wiped his mind clean, erasing the previous thoughts with a well-practised mental sweep.

Colin Harvey closed the door behind him. The rest of the day until his work was finished would belong to Detective-Inspector Colin Harvey, attached to the Number 22 Regional Crime Squad. He had joined the squad a month before from the County force on a two-year attachment. It had been awkward at first, adapting himself to the city and its ways, modifying his training with the County CID, to meet the more rigid demands of the Regional Squad. He set off along the cream-walled corridor, listening to the already familiar sounds of the police headquarters, the flat drone of the loudspeaker in the control-room; the typewriters clattering in the side offices. Harvey turned at the staircase and went up to the squad offices on the second floor.

Leric was waiting for him in the general office, sitting on the edge of the DI's desk, drinking a cup of tea and flipping through one of the morning newspapers.

'Mornin'.' Leric put the cup down and stood up.

Harvey smiled at the Detective-Sergeant's greeting. 'If this is the best you city blokes can do, I think I'll ask for a transfer.' He pulled the duty book across his desk and signed it.

'You'll get used to it, the first ten years are the worst.'

Leric had joined the squad at the same time as Harvey, but he had moved from the city force, from the City Crime Squad in fact, where his duties had been very similar to those of the Regional.

'Once your lungs get used to the fug and your nerves don't twitch every time you boot a door in, then you can say you've arrived.'

Harvey shrugged, flipped through the pile of reports in his in-tray and looked at his watch again. The morning conference was at 9.30. Three detectives, officers of the stand-by crew, were already working, one had a telephone cradled to his ear and the other two were conferring over a grey filing cabinet, which contained the MO file. Harvey glanced down the open page of the duty book. The other crews were already out on current crime inquiries.

'The gaffer's in.' Leric nodded at the fluted glass panel at the end of the long room next to a door marked Co-ordinator. 'I reckon there's something on. Harry Landon's been in with him for over half an hour.'

'He was your guvnor, wasn't he?'

Leric nodded. He was about to speak when the internal telephone on the desk buzzed and Harvey picked up the receiver. 'DI Harvey, sir.' A pause. 'Right away.' He put the phone down. 'Looks as if you'll find out now, Leric. He wants us.'

Leric pulled a face. 'Well, we're the new boys, so I suppose we've got it coming . . .'

Harvey buttoned his jacket and straightened the knot of his tie. Sometimes Leric's acid attitude rattled him, but there was no point in reprimanding the sergeant. He had a distinct advantage over Harvey which had nothing to

Spauling had finished with them in the workshop behind his second-hand car showroom. It would have been too much for Spauling to handle on his own, and besides he didn't have the contacts to keep the underworld export routes open by himself. With Mace's help, cars stolen in the city were slipped into the workshop where their identities were changed, a re-spray job completed and then they were moved to the docks and shipped quietly to the Continent in exchange for a consignment of stolen Mercedes and Fiats to go on sale in the showroom. Mace took a cut of the deal and Spauling's mechanics and drivers were picked more for their brawn than their brains, ten hard men, always available when the firm needed them. It was all part of the arrangement.

This was the first time, thought Farrow, as he drove across, that he had needed Spauling's help since Mace went down, and he would feel easier with Ted's lads to back him up if there was to be trouble.

On the surface, Spauling was a respectable motor dealer, and he took care to keep up his image. As Farrow turned the Jaguar into a quiet suburban road, tree-lined and peaceful, with the detached houses set well back from the roadway, secluded behind sculptured hedges, he had a mental picture of the crooked car dealer cutting the lawns on a Sunday morning and playing a round of golf with his stockbroker neighbours. You wouldn't have thought Ted was a villain.

He turned the car into the tarmac drive which swept alongside a long lawn and opened into a parking space beside the two-car garage and in front of the Cotswold stone porch of the Spauling home.

'Stay in the car, Miller. I'm going to have a chat with Ted . . .' It was better that Miller kept out of it, better

C

the details didn't get reported back to Mace; even in prison, he could stick his oar in and Barney wanted room to breathe.

Farrow stood in the porch and listened to the chiming bell inside the house. He saw the figure moving along the hallway through the glazed front door, a blur on the ripple glass.

'Hallo, Irene . . .'

The woman smiled. Irene Spauling stood at the open door and touched her platinum blonde hair with her free hand. 'Well, well, Barney Farrow, you're a stranger.' She leaned an arm on the door and smiled at him with lips rather too wide on an already full face. 'Come to keep me company while Ted's away?'

'Ted's away?' Farrow echoed, and she laughed low in her throat.

'Yes, of course. You're a caution, Barney Farrow, you know damn well he's away. He's doing a job for you, isn't he?' She clapped a hand over her mouth in mock alarm. 'Or shouldn't I know little secrets like that?'

Farrow felt a sudden chill, and tried to stop the surprise registering on his face. But the woman had noticed.

'Look, Barney, act your age, I'm his wife, you know. I'm not going to say anything. So Ted doesn't tell me in so many words, but you think I don't know when he's going on a job?' She turned down the corners of her mouth in a fleeting pout. 'I've lived with him long enough. When those two men called for him yesterday, he just said, "I'll be away for a few days, love, don't worry." I've heard it all before. Now, are you coming in for a drink, or are you bothered about the neighbours?' The smile was back.

There was no sense in alarming her, thought Farrow,

Spauling wouldn't have gone anywhere without telling him, that was the understanding. Something had gone wrong, and that made him uneasy.

'No, thanks, Irene, another time perhaps.'

She put a hand on his arm, concern suddenly showing in her eyes. 'Nothing's happened, has it, Barney? He's not in any trouble with the law?'

'No, everything's fine . . .'

'I was a bit worried. I'd never seen the two men before. Are they new?'

'What did they look like?'

'Big built, snappy dressers. They'd got a blue van with them. They asked to see Ted and they all went into the front room for about a quarter of an hour, then he left with them.'

'Don't worry, Irene, it's all right. Ask Ted to give me a ring when he gets back.'

'You won't be seeing him, then?'

Farrow bit his lip. 'Depends, but you give him the message, eh, just in case.'

He said goodbye to Spauling's wife and walked back to the car, conscious that she was watching him from the doorway. He had handled it badly and she had seen that he was worried. He slipped behind the wheel and started the engine. Miller had been watching too.

'What's up now, Barney?'

'I dunno.' The heavy brows masked Farrow's eyes— 'but there's something moving. Spauling's gone missing.'

Farrow stopped the car at the first telephone-box he came to and made three calls which only added to the uneasiness which was welling inside him. Spauling's top henchmen had disappeared too.

CHAPTER IV

OTHERS WERE INTERESTED in the fact that Ted Spauling
was no longer around. They had searched the city for a
week, checking his usual haunts, mentioning the name to
those who made a modest living by the dangerous business of peddling underworld information, and had drawn
a blank.

Veitch and McKenzie were both young men, but already possessed of patience beyond their years. They
checked and double-checked where others might have
given up, but finally they had to admit that Spauling was
going to be a difficult man to find. They went back to the
Regional Squad Headquarters and typed up their nega-
tive reports, because whatever his personal views might
be, a detective-constable just does what he's told.

Harvey accepted the news dispassionately. It was just
one more name to add to the growing list of villains who
had suddenly gone out of circulation in the city. Throughout the week, Harvey and Leric had been working on the
club owners, the gamblers and the croupiers, sounding
them out gently to set up contacts in the club world. It
was slow, tedious work. The only interesting feature of the
whole week was that Sand and Crouper were back in the
city, and someone had bungled. The squad had picked up
the Londoners' Ford Mustang at the city boundary and
had shadowed the distinctive American car into the city.

You wouldn't have thought it was possible to lose a
car like that, but it had happened in the heavy traffic.

For two hours, the squad had cruised the busy streets in the hope of making contact again. They had found the car eventually, parked and empty in a central car park, but there was no sign of the two men who had been in it. Harvey had bawled out the luckless crew, but afterwards the incident was closed, for there was no sense in washing the squad's dirty linen in the close community of the police force. Veitch and McKenzie relieved the officers stationed at the car park.

'Hey, look at this.' Veitch, slouched in the passenger seat of the observation car, was reading a newspaper.

'Look at what?' His partner was watching the Mustang parked on the far side of the car park.

'Here in the paper, it says there were twenty-five house fires in the suburbs last month . . .'

'So?'

'So nothing. I just thought it was interesting, that's all.'

'What's interesting?'

'Well, all those fires. You know, every one means that someone's home got burned.'

'So why are you so interested in fires all of a sudden? How about the month before, you never bothered about that, did you?'

'I've just read it in the paper, that's why. It's a lot of fires. I just thought something ought to be done about it, that's all.'

'Look,' said McKenzie, exasperation creeping into his voice, 'if you're so bloody concerned about it, why don't you transfer to the Fire Brigade?'

Veitch rubbed his chin, apparently considering the suggestion, then his face broke into an impish grin. 'No. I reckon I'd miss hanging around for hours on end with a miserable bastard like you.'

'Miserable! Why, you—' The car radio cut into McKenzie's outburst.

'Alpha Tango to Zebra Four. Regional Crime Squad.'

Veitch unclipped the microphone and acknowledged the car's call sign.

The flat voice from the central information room droned on. 'Zebra Four, DCs Veitch and McKenzie, go to the City General Hospital where a man identified as subject of Regional Crime Squad circulation Number 12 is detained in the Burns Unit.'

Veitch confirmed the message as McKenzie started the car. There was no need to check the circulation. It was Ted Spauling.

'Looks like Ted's had an accident,' said Veitch, replacing the microphone.

'Yeah. Perhaps he got caught in one of those house fires you were on about.'

A relief observation car moved into their parking space as they drove out of the car park and headed towards the hospital.

Although the detectives were still in their twenties, they had seen a good deal of the insides of hospitals, from the road accident carnage of their days in uniform to the victims of rapes, robberies and beatings. They walked in silence along the composition floors of the blank corridors, through the double rubber flaps with the yellowing Perspex windows which took the place of doors, following the signs to the Burns Unit.

Leric was already there, talking to a doctor with the legend 'A Team' embroidered on the breast pocket of his white coat.

The Sergeant nodded a wordless greeting. 'Come on,

the doctor says we can see him for a few minutes before they knock him out. Veitch, come with me and take notes. You pick up his gear, McKenzie, the doctor will show you where it is.'

They went into a small room where the air was heavily charged with the acrid scent of antiseptic. The man lying on the couch was almost enclosed in a polythene envelope connected to an oxygen machine. He was naked, and through the transparent cover the detectives could see the blotched seared flesh, livid and taut on much of the man's torso. His head protruded on to a hard pillow supporting his neck, and beyond the ashen face, the man's lank hair held the lustreless expectancy of death. A nursing sister in a mauve smock adjusted a saline drip in a bedside clamp.

'Third degree burns,' said Leric in a hushed tone. 'Panda man found him sprawled on the pavement, half bloody dead.' He looked down at the figure on the couch. 'The doctor says another ten per cent of the body surface and he would have croaked.'

'What do you reckon happened, Sarge?'

'Someone burned him, that's what happened. Let's try and find out who.' Leric leaned over the figure. 'Hallo, Ted. We've been looking for you.'

The man's eyes were red, shot with ruptured capillaries, and saliva bubbled at the corner of his mouth. Leric could see pain stabbing behind the eyes.

'Leric . . .' the voice was a hoarse whisper and Spauling moved his head so that he could see Veitch standing beside the Sergeant.

'This is Detective Veitch, Ted. We want to know what happened to you.'

The man didn't answer.

'Come on, mate, you don't want them to get away with this, do you? Who burned you?'

Spauling rolled his eyes, his tongue working slowly over the cracked lips. 'Go to hell, coppers . . .'

Leric shook his head. 'That's not very friendly, Ted. Why don't you tell us about it?'

'Look,' Spauling was working hard to form the words. 'Call it an accident . . . You'll get nothing from me.'

The Sergeant leaned closer. 'Grow up, mate. I'll tell you what you're thinking. You think you'll walk out of here and even the score your own way, or else some of your lads will do it for you. Well, I'll tell you something, Ted, if you don't croak, you're going to be in here for a very long time, and as for the rest, I wouldn't be surprised if they aren't getting some of the same medicine. They're not around any more.'

Spauling closed his eyes, and his face contorted as the pain rippled through his body. When he opened them, Leric was holding a hand in front of his face.

'Remember big Eddie with the Mace mob?' Leric closed a finger into his palm. 'He's the first. The rumour is that he had his hand burned off. Then there's your lads . . .' The Sergeant ran through the names, one for each finger. 'They won't be around at visiting time. Someone's putting the squeeze on in this city and they're hitting the villains first. A London mob, is it, Ted? Some of the boys from the Smoke putting the arm on?'

Spauling tried to smile. 'Get knotted . . . just leave me alone. It was an accident, I tell you.'

Leric shrugged. 'Have it your own way, Ted, but remember this: there's still Irene, who's going to look after her? Just think about it. We'll see you again.'

The two detectives went out into the corridor.

'He's a hard case, Sarge.'

'Thinks he is. Perhaps we'll get another crack at him later, he might change his mind.'

McKenzie was waiting for them, carrying a plastic bag in his hand. 'These are his clothes, what's left of them. I've collected up the charred bits too. What happened, did he fall into a furnace?'

Leric lit a cigarette. 'Get the clothes over to the forensic. With a bit of luck, they'll be able to tell us.'

Arrangements were made for an officer to stay on at the hospital to keep a watch over Spauling, and the three detectives went back to the crime squad headquarters.

She was there when they arrived, sitting with her hands in her lap, staring at the untouched cup of tea which Harvey had given her after breaking the news that her husband had been found. Irene Spauling sat in the straight-backed chair in the bare interview room, her platinum hair falling over her face, brushing a frond away from her eyes occasionally with her hand. She sat still and quiet and tears rolled down her cheeks, mixing the mascara with the face powder. She hugged her grief close like a child.

Harvey called Leric into the interview room. 'Sergeant Leric has just come from the hospital, Mrs Spauling.'

She looked up, then turned her gaze back to the tea-cup.

'You should have told me, Irene,' Leric began with a hint of reproach in his voice. 'I've always looked after Ted in the past, haven't I? You should have told me when he went, and we could have stopped it.'

She looked up again, her eyes heavy from crying. 'He told me it would be all right . . . not to worry. It was going to be all right, Ted said so.'

Leric had known the Spaulings over the years. He had seen Ted grow from a small-time thief into the shady car dealer he was today. Sometimes he was careless enough to get caught and he had served several prison sentences, but as he expanded in the underworld, there was never enough evidence to tie Spauling in with the rackets. He wore a mantle of respectability now, and Irene had always been there beside him.

'I told you it was time he packed it in, Irene.' Leric sat opposite the woman. 'He was bound to get hurt one of these days. I told you, too. Now it's happened.'

She didn't speak.

Harvey offered a packet of cigarettes and she took one. The DI held a match to the trembling tip. 'Try not to worry, Mrs Spauling, they'll do all they can for him at the hospital.'

'I must go to him.' Her voice cracked. 'But he can't see me . . . not like this.' She dabbed at the tears with a paper tissue.

'Take it easy, Irene,' said Leric. 'We'll take you to the hospital soon, he'll be in the operating theatre now, so you won't be able to do anything. We want the people who did this to Ted, and the best way you can help is by answering a few questions.'

'Did you see him?' She searched Leric's eyes for some sign, anything.

'Yes, I saw him. He's been burned, Irene, somebody burned him.'

The detectives heard the sharp intake of breath, the gasp, as the shock hit the woman. 'Oh God . . . he's . . .

he's going to live isn't he? I knew he was hurt, but burnt
. . . oh no!'

'The doctors think he'll pull through . . .' Leric sensed
he could catch the woman now while her emotions were
raw, while the code her husband had instilled into her
was shattered by her grief, the code which forbade giving
information to the police. The detective dropped his voice.
'For Ted's sake, Irene, tell us anything you know. When
did he go, and who with?'

'That Barney, I knew there'd been trouble. I told Ted
not to . . .' she caught the words and turned her eyes
back to her folded hands.

'Come on,' said Leric gently. 'Who's Barney? Did Ted
go with him?'

She shook her head. 'I don't know any Barney. I made
a mistake, that's all.'

Leric knew a Barney, though.

'Was it Barney Farrow, Irene? You might as well tell
us. Was it?'

'I . . . I don't know . . .'

Harvey chipped in. 'Did he burn your husband, Mrs
Spauling? Did he do a terrible thing like that?'

'Don't . . .' She shook her head as if to escape the
detective's questions.

'They'll be back to finish it, Irene—' Leric kept it up—
'when they know he's still alive. They'll have to, and then
you'll be alone.'

The woman held her head in her hands, the bright red
nails clutching at her hair. 'Stop it, stop it . . .' She was
close to breaking-point. 'Barney came after, he was looking for Ted,' she sobbed. 'Two men I'd never seen before
came to the house. He went away with them.'

Great sobs racked Irene Spauling's body as she slumped

in the chair in the tiny interview room. The detectives waited as she calmed herself, both knowing that the moment had passed.

'We want you to look at some pictures and see if you recognize any of them,' said Harvey at last.

He showed her the CRO portraits one at a time while Leric studied her face. She shook her head imperceptibly as each record card was held up. Harvey showed her the pictures of the Londoners, Sand and Crouper, and Leric would have sworn there was a flicker of recognition in the woman's eyes, but perhaps it was just wishful thinking. Harvey dropped the last card on to the pile on the desk and asked her if she could identify anyone. Irene Spauling shook her head without speaking, and the DI picked up the telephone and asked for one of the squad's women detectives to take Mrs Spauling to the hospital.

When she had gone, the two policemen gathered in the shreds of information.

'What do you know about this character Barney, then, Leric?'

The Sergeant chewed on a matchstick. 'He's just a villain, gaffer, like the rest. Jack Mace was the strong man in town until he went to prison and Barney Farrow was his right arm.'

'He's got a legitimate business I suppose?'

'Oh yes—that's what put Jack in the fairy. They're partners in a wholesale fruit firm, supplying the markets here and in Manchester. They've got warehouses at the markets; when we had a look at one here, it was stuffed full of nicked furs. Jack copped his corner, bang to rights, so now he's doing time.'

'And now the London boys think the field's wide open again. Is that what you think?'

'Looks like it. Perhaps Farrow sold out to the other side.'

'Why would he do that? From what I've heard, you couldn't get a thing on the Mace mob that would stand up in court. With Mace inside, Farrow would be able to carry on as before.'

'Perhaps they made him a good offer to step aside.'

'So why did he go round to see Irene Spauling if he knew they were working over her husband?'

Leric dropped the match into the ashtray. 'Perhaps he fancies her.'

Harvey leaned back in his chair, rubbing his eyes with the back of his hands. 'I think it's time we had a little chat with Barney Farrow. Take a couple of the lads and fetch him in.'

'He might be hard to find, like Spauling.'

'No, I don't think so. There's a pattern coming out of this, Leric. Spauling's clinched it. They're knocking off the labourers first. Farrow's time is yet to come.'

'What if I can't find him, gaffer?'

Harvey smiled. 'I don't think that'll happen, do you? It wouldn't do much for your rep if you came back empty-handed, now would it?'

The taunt left a shadow over Leric's face. His reply was stiff : 'If he's in town, I'll find him—sir.'

'I'll be waiting.'

Harvey watched the Sergeant leave the office, and then began the tedious task of re-reading every statement in the file. He needed the details at his fingertips.

CHAPTER V

THEY BEGAN with the pubs, from the back street taverns to the hotel cocktail bars, asking the same question, picking up snippets of information from their informers. Occasionally Leric would go into the bar alone, more often, he would take Veitch with him. McKenzie always stayed behind the wheel of the crime car, for it was Leric's policy never to crowd his sarbuts with too much law.

It was late evening when the police car stopped outside the You-Too Club in Park Street, a casino where the food and drink were thrown in free as long as the customers were spending money at the tables. They had been told that Farrow would almost certainly be there, for the whisper said he was looking after one of the hostesses.

Leric pressed the bell set in the heavy studded door, and a peephole opened in the otherwise solid oak panels.

'Police—open up.' Leric held his warrant card up to the face which had appeared in the small opening.

The door opened and a man in a midnight blue mohair suit with a shock of blond hair falling over his forehead stood in the entrance.

'Well—well, Mr Leric.' The doorman was grinning. 'Is this a business or a social call?'

Leric, his raincoat open and his hands thrust in his trouser pockets, nodded over his shoulder to Veitch. 'Remember the face, Veitch . . . Max Lincoln, sometimes known as Max the Chiv. He's got a form sheet as long as your arm. Wounding, Section 18, robbery with violence, possession of an offensive weapon. He's a nasty anti-social little thug, and besides that, he dyes his hair. He's as queer as a clockwork orange, so don't bend down or turn your back on him.'

The doorman was still grinning. 'That's not very nice, Mr Leric. The prison headshrinker said I just wasn't adjusted, that's all.'

'You want to keep your crummy job, son?' Leric stepped into the doorway.

The grin disappeared. 'Now wait a minute, gents. I got to tell the boss the law's here. You got a warrant?'

'Just spend a couple of minutes powdering your nose and forget you saw us, or we might take a closer look at this flea-pit and stick a raid on the place. Now the boss wouldn't like that, would he?'

'There's not going to be any bother, is there?'

'Not if you get out of the way,' replied Leric. 'We just want a quiet look around, that's all.'

Lincoln grinned again. 'Well, why didn't you say so? You know you're always welcome here, Mr Leric, you and your friends.' He included Veitch in the invitation. He gave a broad wink, stepped aside and bowed with exaggerated courtesy, ushering the detectives into the club foyer. 'Just don't frighten the customers, that's all, gents. We like to keep a friendly atmosphere here, and some people scare easily.'

Leric and Veitch walked past the doorman and into the club.

The bar was dimly lit and the handful of drinkers who had broken off from the gaming tables were watching a colour television set from easy-chairs scattered around the room. A series of open arches separated the lounge from the bar itself, where a bald-headed man in a white waiter's coat was leaning on his elbows, intent on the TV show.

Leric slipped on to one of the high stools and Veitch leaned beside him. The barman dragged himself away from the screen and approached them, but no one else took any notice.

'Quiet night?' asked Leric conversationally.

'Always is, Wednesday. What you drinking, gents?'

'Two halves of bitter,' said Leric.

The barman pulled the toggle of the beer pump, steadying two glasses below the nozzle. Veitch took out a packet of cigarettes, handed one to the Sergeant and lit them as Leric glanced around the room. The barman busied himself with the drinks.

'No sign of Barney Farrow in here, then,' Leric remarked to the young detective. Veitch shook his head, puzzled that the Sergeant should have mentioned the name while the barman was still in earshot. The man placed the two beers on the bar.

'That'll be two and eight.'

Leric took some change from his pocket, a pound note and some coins. 'Have one yourself?'

The barman scratched his ear. 'Thanks, I'll have a half.' He turned to the pump again, watching the beer gurgle into the glass. 'They say there's a good wrestling match on at the Empire tonight.'

Leric picked up his glass and downed the drink in two long swallows. 'Worth seeing, is it?' He pushed the tumbler across the bar top and Veitch could see that the Sergeant had dropped a pound note into the empty glass. He busied himself with his own drink.

'I'd say it'd be right up your street,' offered the barman conversationally. 'Some big names on the bill.'

Leric jingled his change.

'With yours, that'll be four bob, then.' The Sergeant handed two coins to the barman who had already collected the empty glass. Leric turned to Veitch. 'You fit, mate? No sense in hanging about here.'

Veitch drained his glass, gulping the last mouthful. They had been drinking steadily since this search for Farrow had begun and his head was beginning to swim. Leric set a crippling pace, downing drink after drink, and he was already off the stool, retracing his steps to the lobby. The barman had resumed his viewing pose at the end of the bar, and Veitch followed the Sergeant, wondering if his beer-fogged brain had missed some important point.

Lincoln met them at the door, turning from the full-length mirror in which he had been combing his hair. 'Leaving so soon, are we?' He grinned. 'What's the matter, boys? Is the beer off?'

Leric pulled a face. 'You call that cat's pee beer? We just wanted to make sure you hadn't got a couple of brasses in the back room, that's all.'

'Well, really.' Lincoln affected a shocked expression. 'You must be joking, Mr Leric. This is a respectable club.'

'I'll bet,' said Leric drily. 'No competition allowed, eh?'

The doorman's face puffed with sudden anger. 'There's such a thing as slander, you know.'

Leric moved past him and opened the door. 'Get stuffed, Lincoln, you make me sick.' He stepped out on to the pavement with Veitch, and the door slammed behind them.

Leric looked at his watch as they walked back to the police Westminster. It was almost nine o'clock. The wrestling tournament would have started at 7.30 and would end about half past ten, there was still plenty of time. Veitch had fallen into step beside him, and Leric, immersed in his own thoughts and plans, was suddenly surprised to hear the young detective speak.

'I thought we were going to have a look round the club, Sarge.' There was a truculent tone in the young man's voice. 'We didn't even go into the gaming rooms.' Some of the words were gently slurred.

Leric stopped, the wind whipping his mackintosh as he reached the police car. He looked sharply at Veitch. 'You've been on the wobble too long tonight, my lad, it's addled your brain.'

'But you said . . .' Veitch swayed a little and Leric peered closely at him. There was a film of sweat standing out on the lad's forehead and his eyes were pink and watery. What was he, middle twenties perhaps? Leric paused. The drinking was part of the job, it was where you got your information, chatted up your sarbuts, softened up Chummy, and a half-cut detective was no bloody use at all. Veitch was young yet and he would learn to hold his liquor, learn the way every other detective learned, if he was going to make the grade, by long, demanding, elbow-bending hours at the bars of countless pubs. It was part of the job.

'When you're on the beer,' said Leric slowly, recalling the words of a long-departed mentor, 'keep half your mind for drinking and the other half for thinking. Until you can do that, son, don't ask stupid questions.'

He slipped into the front seat beside McKenzie, who had been waiting in the car.

'Where to now, Sarge?'

'The Empire. We're going to watch some wrestling, that's if your mate can stay awake long enough.' Leric jerked his thumb to the back seat, but his sarcasm was wasted on Veitch, who had opened the window and was gulping in the cool night air.

They drove across the city, the big car weaving through the traffic, always heavy except for a short lull in the early hours of the morning, when the streets snatched a brief respite before the rush hour. The Empire was a converted cinema which had been given a face lift and transformed into a sporting club, and because it commanded a prime position in the city centre, the moguls who owned it had tried to inject a veneer of class into the new entertainment. The Empire Sporting Club, with a 20 guinea a year membership, had been in existence for over two years, and the patrons still wore dinner-jackets at the insistence of the management.

The Westminster cruised along a row of parked cars and McKenzie stopped on the white-painted cross between the meter bays, which was reserved for the Panda Patrol. This time Leric decided that Veitch should stay in the car and he walked with McKenzie to the softly lit foyer of the club. The uniformed commissionaire was waiting just inside the entrance and he stepped out as they approached, appraising them haughtily. He was a new man to Leric, who had seen them come and go.

'I'm sorry, gentlemen.' The commissionaire held out an arm as the detectives stepped on to the plush carpet. 'Members only, it's a rule of the club.'

Leric flipped open his warrant card, and asked for the club manager. 'Police officers. We want to see Mr Saunders.'

The man's expression didn't change. 'May I ask for what purpose, sir? Mr Saunders is very busy. Perhaps you could come back later, when it's more convenient.'

Leric smiled sweetly. 'We'd very much like to see him now.'

'I'm afraid that won't be possible, sir. The programme hasn't finished.'

Leric was rapidly tiring of the man's attitude and his bloody plum in the mouth voice. 'Look,' said the Sergeant, 'This is Detective-Constable McKenzie. Now you go inside and get Mr Saunders out here, and do it quickly, or else—' he nodded at McKenzie standing beside him— 'my colleague here will run out of patience and nick you for obstructing the police.'

The commissionaire's eyes widened, he went to reply, thought better of it and turned towards his cubbyhole. Leric watched him go inside and begin talking into a telephone.

'Jumped-up git,' he murmured to McKenzie, and the young officer grinned. Within two minutes Saunders appeared, rubbing his hands and plainly worried. They went with him to his office and explained that they were looking for someone, discreetly of course, and on the understanding that they wouldn't upset any of the members, the two detectives were allowed to stand at the rear of the auditorium near to the exit.

The interior of the big hall, with tiers of seats sloping down to the brilliantly lit square ring at the centre, was wreathed in cigar smoke and heavy with the cadence of male voice. Leric searched the audience expertly, taking advantage of the fact that everyone's attention was on the ring where two bull-necked heavyweights were seeking to break each other's backs with the maximum of showmanship.

He picked out Farrow in the third row, head bent in conversation with a young man whose shoulder-muscles almost burst his jacket, and who occasionally scratched the top of his cropped head.

'That's me laddo,' Leric told McKenzie, indicating Farrow. 'Over there by the aisle. Keep your eye on him. We'll catch him when he comes out.'

There were two more bouts and the detectives waited, smoking in the shadows by the curtained exit. One of the staff opened the doors as the MC stepped into the ring to wind up the evening's entertainment. Pretty soon the audience was leaving, joking, laughing, discussing the fights. Leric spotted Farrow leave his seat and make his way to the cloakroom. He signalled to McKenzie, and they began to elbow their way through the sea of dinner-jackets towards the men's room. There was no sign of Farrow in the cloakroom, and Leric pushed through to the gents' with McKenzie behind him. They found Farrow in the urinal, relieving himself. Leric stepped up beside him.

'Hallo, Barney.'

Farrow glanced sideways and his eyes narrowed with recognition. 'Well, well, Leric . . . I didn't know you were a member.'

'We've been looking all over town for you, Barney.'

Farrow continued to urinate. 'What for? I've done nothing.'

Leric chuckled. 'Nobody said you had.'

'Then what?'

'New bloke down at the nick, Inspector Harvey. He'd like a chat with you, Barney.'

'I suppose there's no harm in a chat, is there, mate? So he's sent you out on the errand-boy job, eh?' A touch of sarcasm.

Cool customer, Leric thought, not a flicker there, no

surprise, not even a lifted eyebrow. 'Something like that,' replied the detective. 'He's waiting. It won't take a minute.'

Farrow stepped back, adjusted his zip and almost bumped into McKenzie. 'This your lad?'

'Yes,' Leric said.

'He must want to see me pretty bad, this Inspector Harvey.'

'Like I said, he's waiting.'

Farrow shrugged. 'My car's outside. I'll follow you, then.'

No questions, none of the police persecution chat, or the old 'why can't you leave me alone, I'm a respectable citizen now' about this merchant, thought Leric. Very cool. 'I'll come with you, if it's all the same to you, Barney. Just so you don't get lost on the way.'

Farrow smiled without mirth.

As they left the Empire and walked across the car park, Leric decided to say nothing at all to Farrow about the inquiry and the reason why they had sought him out. He wanted the man completely unprepared, and was looking forward to the prospect of the new DI, Colin Harvey, fresh from the fields and the haystacks, confronting a city villain. He wanted to see how Harvey would handle a real criminal, for Leric had a hearty contempt for the county coppers and their preoccupation with the petty crime which was all they had to bother about. So far he had been a buffer, mixing with the criminals and leaving Harvey to his paper work. Now he would see the Inspector's true colours and he savoured the prospect of the confrontation.

Farrow opened the passenger door of the blue Jaguar and Leric slipped into the soft leather seat.

'Doing all right, eh, Barney?' Leric looked apprecia-tively around the luxurious interior of the car. 'Not like the old days on the market wagons.'

Farrow started the engine. 'Can't grumble,' he replied non-committally, turning out of the car park and follow-ing the twin tail-lights of the Westminster, which had intercepted them at the exit ramp. 'It's on the business. Tax relief.' Farrow knew all about the seemingly inno-cent questions which suddenly jumped together like the jaws of a trap and left you caught, condemned by an unguarded word. Too many D's had tried it on with him. He would give nothing away.

'Doing all right, then—the business?' Leric kept up the flippant chat.

'So-so.' Farrow concentrated on his driving.

'Still send the odd box of fruit round to the local nick, Barney?'

Farrow glanced sideways at his passenger. 'The old days are past, Leric. If I did that now, some bright lad would nick me for attempted bribery. It's been a long time since you showed your face in the markets.'

Leric smiled. 'Times change, Barney, you move on and old faces get forgotten.'

Leric could still remember his first encounter with Barney Farrow, back in his early days as a probationary constable working from the dingy police station, just around the corner from the city markets. Farrow and Jack Mace had been barrow-boys with a pitch in the raw down-to-earth atmosphere of the markets, building their reputation among the local villains with their wits and their fists.

'How'd you know I was at the fights?'

'We asked.' Leric was enjoying the banter and he

steered the conversation back into trivia. Why should he make it easy for Harvey by telling this man why they had picked him up? 'Hear you fancy one of the club birds, Barney.'

Farrow caught the drift as well. He was content to wait. He had one rule of thumb for dealing with coppers —say nothing and keep a straight face while you're saying it. He just chuckled. 'Angela, you mean . . . that's no secret.'

Was it the way Farrow had said the name, almost with a leer, or was it just that his mind was relaxed and un-prepared for the sudden jolt, like a hard doubled fist in the solar plexus? Was it just the name, coming suddenly unexpected like that, the name of his wife who had di-vorced him two years ago?

The job had broken his marriage. Leric would come home in the early hours, bone weary from endless observa-tion duty; stinking of drink from a night on the beer, trailing some tearaway; unshaven and sweat-stained from long interrogation sessions when they had a suspect inside. He would crawl into bed dead beat, and in the end there was nothing to talk about. Once she had even sent his underclothes to the Forensic Lab, after accusing him of keeping a mistress. Finally, their marriage was dissolved on the grounds of cruelty. Leric let her go and didn't defend the case; now his attitude towards the job reflected the bitterness he felt at the loss of a normal home life.

Angela. Farrow concentrated on his driving, glad of the lull in the conversation. It gave him a chance to clear his thoughts.

So the D's were on to Angela, were they? It had always been the same, brief affairs with women whose second names he could no longer remember, whose faces ran into a blur when he tried to recall them. Farrow knew he could never allow himself a normal emotional relationship with any of them, for it would leave him vulnerable; he couldn't afford the luxury of a home life. He had used the threat himself without hesitation when a persuader was needed: 'Your missus, Danny boy, all right, is she?' A half smile to let it sink in. 'You wouldn't like her to get hurt, now would you?' The thought of exposing himself to that kind of risk chilled him. No, he would never love anyone, it just wasn't worth it.

There were plenty of girls in the clubs out for a good time, not caring if he would be around tomorrow, or if it would be someone else's head on the pillow. As long as your wallet was fat enough, they were there for the taking, and Farrow had got used to buying what he wanted. Do unto others before they do unto you, do it faster, harder and without feeling, because if you falter just once, you'll end up bleeding to death in an alley with your stomach hanging out.

Farrow had learned the code of the underworld one night a long time ago, crouching beside Mace in a dark warehouse, breathing his own fear, waiting for a rival mob outside to make their move. They were using bolt cutters on the double doors and he could hear their soft curses over the sound of the rain drumming on the roof. 'Keep still,' Mace whispered, 'wait your chance.' The fight which followed had been the toughest round in their bid for control of the city's underworld, but Farrow's recollection of the night was hazy, for in the course of the battle his throat had been torn by a knife blade. The wound had healed slowly and painfully, with little medical attention. Farrow remembered recovering con-

sciousness in the cellar of the terraced house where Mace
lived, and throughout the following days he drifted in and
out of reality. For months after that night he was unable
to talk, for the thin blade had penetrated his larynx, and
the knife had left its mark, a ragged scar shaped like an
oak leaf. The Mace mob had crushed the opposition and
founded its reputation on violence.

Afterwards Farrow had lived alone, in flats and rooms,
never far from the makeshift homes of his companions.
He had learned to dodge the law, moving on before the
D's could find him. Living out of suitcases more often
than not. As the Mace empire grew, he took to renting
luxury flats in different parts of the city, moving from
one to another so that no one, his own kind or the law,
would know where to find him. He grew to resent Mace
for the power and authority he held in the underworld.
Nobody argued with Jack Mace and got away with it,
he had the guts and the contacts to stay on top. Farrow
spat out of the open car window. Jack Mace had prickled
under his skin long enough.

CHAPTER VI

COLIN HARVEY closed the clip folder, dropped it on his
desk, leaned back in his chair and rubbed his eyes. The
crime squad office was in darkness except for the pool of
light from the globe over his desk; silent except for the
noise of night traffic outside and the hum of the extractor
fan on the wall.

The bulky file held typed transcripts of notebooks made
up after every interview since the team was formed a

month ago. There were no signed statements, nothing which would stand up in court, just the gist of word of mouth conversations between the detectives, their informants and the criminals they had sought out. Almost every entry carried the footnote : 'The above cannot be substantiated by any witness.'

Harvey pushed the file aside. As the investigating officer he had kept a close watch on its daily progress and the watching and waiting had not been wasted, but even so, it was a strange experience for the Detective-Inspector. With his old force, he had been schooled differently. More often than not, if criminals fought among themselves, the police were content to let them sort it out and then pick up the pieces afterwards. Leave 'em alone until they've broken each others' heads and then stick an affray charge on the lot of them. But the regional squad was more interested in the criminals than the crime, and so they had worked on, trying to forecast the motive for the Londoners' sudden interest in the city; the reason why notorious local villains had mysteriously disappeared; the beatings and the reluctance of once reliable contacts to be seen talking to a detective; the threats and the attempted bribes.

They were all detailed in the file and the outcome seemed obvious enough even to Harvey, who knew he still had a lot to learn about city criminals and their ways. It was a terror campaign, subtle, subversive to begin with, violent and ruthless when necessary, which would mushroom into a full-scale take-over battle in the underworld. But because of its very nature, criminals against criminals within the confines of their own society, the police could not hope to prove a word of it, yet.

He felt for a cigarette in the jacket draped over the

back of his chair and pushed his shirt-sleeves up above the elbows on his freckled forearms, which would have looked more at home on a farmer than a policeman. He lit the cigarette and dropped the match into the overflowing ashtray, reflecting that he was smoking far too heavily since he had joined the squad. They would wait their time, the Londoners, content to pick off the opposition one by one, recruit their own organization from the hangers-on, the thrill kids and the tearaways on the fringe of the underworld, who would do the dirty work for whoever was in power. Those who resisted would be conscripted by threat, or eliminated, depending on their worth. They were coming for their cut from the night-clubs and the casinos where the bent money, the proceeds of crime, circulated. They would bear down on the pimps and the brasses who worked for them, on the crime, the vice and the corruption. They would grow fat and power-ful; shady businessmen would pay for protection and the mob would grasp out greedily, undermining and insinuating their way into business circles until prominent public figures fell into their hands, powerless to protest. Sand, Crouper and the rest whose names they still had to learn.

Harvey looked up and pushed the thoughts aside. A crystal ball was no part of his job, he needed facts. He reached across for the telephone and waited for the switchboard to answer. 'National Line, please.' The girl's bored voice was replaced with the dialling tone. He called his wife at home. After telling her he would prob-ably be working very late, he listened patiently to her account of the day's happenings. When he finally replaced the receiver, he was satisfied that the framework of his life had not changed.

Footsteps broke the silence, the door opened and Leric walked into the room. The Sergeant was smiling.

He nodded at the case file on Harvey's desk. 'You'll need more than that for Barney Farrow, gaffer. If you think he's going to come in here and kiss your arse, forget it.'

'Where is he?'

Leric jerked a thumb at the darkened doorway. 'I've got him downstairs.'

Harvey rubbed his chin. 'Any trouble?'

'No, he's too old a hand for that. I just wheeled him in like you said. He didn't even ask what it was about.'

'Have you talked to him, on the way?'

'No, I thought I'd leave that to you,' said Leric with a wider grin.

Colin Harvey caught the inference, but let it go. He was too weary to play games with the city Sergeant who was just waiting his chance to catch him out. 'All right,' he said heavily, 'let's have it. Where did you get on to him?'

Leric took off his mackintosh and dropped it on a near-by desk. 'We caught up with him at the Empire, watching the wrestling. He's been a perfect gentleman ever since.'

Harvey stood up and stretched his cramped muscles, then turned to the window. The outline of the brick wall across the air shaft was just visible. He counted the first row to relax his mind, and turned to Leric. 'I'm going to freshen up a bit. Keep him happy for a minute, will you, Sergeant, then bring him up.'

Leric frowned. 'It'd be better done in the interview room, gaffer. We could lean on him harder down there. Sort of keep a bit of an advantage, if you see what I mean.'

Harvey opened the bottom drawer of his desk and took out a battery shaver then reached for his jacket. 'Nobody's going to do any leaning, Leric. Just bring him up, that's all.'

Leric shrugged. 'It won't do you any good. These villains only understand one thing.'

'I'll remember that. You just bring him up here.'

What's he think this is, thought Leric stubbornly, a bloody tea-party? Still, it's his own funeral. Barney Farrow'll mark him down for a right sucker. Let him get on with it, then. 'Shall I get one of the DCs to take the notes, gaffer?'

Harvey turned at the doorway, his jacket over his arm. 'No, let them book off. You don't want to miss anything, do you? You can take the notes yourself.'

Leric was shocked. 'Well, I thought I'd be in on the questioning. I mean, I know the bloke and you don't. I can't do that and take the notes as well.'

'That's right, you can't, can you?' Harvey paused with his hand on the door knob. 'In that case, you just leave the talking to me, eh, and keep on your toes. I want his answers verbátim.'

The bloody nerve, a jumped-up inspector from the sticks. Why, I've knocked off more villains than he's had hot dinners. Choking with indignation, Leric stood speechless as the Inspector closed the door behind him.

Harvey walked down the corridor to the gents', deep in thought. Leric was right, of course; he didn't know the man and the Sergeant would probably have been a useful aide for the questioning session which was to follow, but he was getting just a little sick of the condescending attitude of the city detective, and besides, he had a few ideas of his own on how Barney Farrow could contribute to the inquiry. It was time he made a stand.

Harvey let himself into the washroom, ran the cold water tap over his wrists and felt the coolness coursing through his bloodstream. He washed his face carefully and then shaved, peering at his reflection in the mirror. Although it was well into spring, the central heating in the police station was still operating, and at times, the detectives on the second-floor offices of the Regional squad were forced to work in stifling conditions. The rooms had been designed as store space before the pressure of accommodation had impelled the police to convert them into offices; consequently there were no windows which opened, and the partitioning which divided off the long room just acted as a heat trap.

As he had read through the Incident File that night, Harvey had noticed the stale air in the room and the lassitude which came with it. On several occasions he had gone out into the corridor to snatch a breath of fresh air before resuming the tedious work at his desk. For some reason which only the architects who designed the building could know, at this time of the year the squad offices were even hotter at night than they were during the day.

He turned from the wash-basin refreshed, competent again and ready to work another eight hours if need be. He had developed a technique for ridding his body of hunger, fatigue, depression or minor irritations. Now he could put them aside when necessary, wipe his mind clean like a slate, the way he did every morning when he arrived at the station. He was ready to face Barney Farrow.

Harvey rolled down his sleeves, buttoned the cuffs and

slipped into his jacket. He refastened the neck button of
his shirt and pulled the knot of his tie back into place. He
checked his appearance once more in the mirror, rubbed
his palms over his hair and walked back down the corridor to the squad room.

He knew he would get nothing from Farrow for any
altruistic reasons, but he hoped the confrontation would
give him an insight into the man's personality. Farrow
was Jack Mace's partner, heir to the throne in the Mace
underworld. Sooner or later he would have to show his
hand, and Harvey wanted to be able to put himself in
his shoes when the time came.

He reached the glass-ribbed door of the general office
and stepped inside the room, the lines of concentrated
thought erased from his brow and his eyes clear and un-
troubled. He wanted to start with Farrow on at least
equal terms.

The single light still burned over the DI's desk leaving
much of the office in shadow. Harvey closed the door
behind him and Leric rose from the chair he had arranged
inside the pool of light. The Sergeant nodded to the man
sitting at the far side of the desk.

'This is Barney Farrow, sir.' Harvey could detect a surly
note in Leric's voice, but his attention was on the third
man in the room.

Farrow sat smoking, arms resting on his knees, leaning
slightly forward in the chair, the cigarette hanging in a
limp hand. Harvey recognized him from the description :
the lean face, heavy eyebrows, deep-set eyes, a face which
would be difficult to forget. He knew the scar would be
there too, below the line of the man's collar, most probably. It had all been on the CRO card.

They were waiting for him, expectant, Leric half hopeful that he would make a fool of himself, Farrow—well, he would soon find out. Harvey dropped into his own chair, brisk, businesslike, mindless of the heavy air in the room.

'Barney Farrow, a couple of convictions for minor crime and one for violence, but that was a long time ago, wasn't it?' Harvey smiled. 'Why do you think I want to see you, Mr Farrow?'

The man shrugged. 'Suppose you tell me.'

Colin Harvey noted the voice, gruff from the effects of the knife wound. He waved a hand around the office. 'We've stayed open especially for you tonight, Mr Farrow. We wanted to see you rather badly.'

'OK, I'm here, now what?'

'Still no idea why we've gone to all this trouble?'

'How would I know?'

'Remember Ted Spauling, Mr Farrow?' Harvey held up his hand. 'Don't bother to answer that; let me tell you. He was a friend of yours, more a colleague. Well, Mr Spauling seems to have suffered a most unfortunate accident.'

Farrow puffed on his cigarette. 'So what's it got to do with me?'

'We wanted to see you before anything like that happened to you.'

'Why should it? Look, Mr Harvey, I'm a businessman. Spauling did some haulage work for me from time to time, that's all.'

Harvey tapped the file in front of him. 'You've got some other friends too—Eddie Roach, for instance. Eddie worked in your warehouse as a fruit porter, only he

E

doesn't seem to be around any more. We haven't seen Eddie for a week or two, and we're told he also had rather a nasty accident. Lost a hand, didn't he?'

'You've been listening to too much gossip, Mr Harvey. Eddie Roach left my firm a month ago. I gave him his cards myself. He said he was going abroad—Merchant Navy if I recall right.'

Harvey nodded. 'That's alright, Mr Farrow. We aren't bothered too much about Eddie.'

Harvey took a typed list from the file and slowly read out a group of names, pausing after each one to ask Farrow about the man in question. After half an hour he had completed the list and Farrow was still non-committal.

Harvey watched the man closely, saw the beads of perspiration forming on his brow, his discomfort as the sweat soaked into his clothes. Leric's face glistened too, but the Sergeant stuck doggedly to his notebook, recording every word of Farrow's replies.

After a while Harvey placed the list back in the file. 'Well now, there seems to be nothing to connect you with any of these people, but the fact is that some of them have disappeared, others have been beaten up, and one or two of them seem to have something on their mind. Take Alan Harper, for instance, the car salesman. One of my officers went round to his home on a purely routine matter and Harper offered to pay him £300 to forget it. Now why do you think he did that?'

'How would I know? The name means nothing to me.' Farrow was trying hard to preserve his patience. What did this copper think he was playing at, bringing him into an empty police station late at night, asking a lot of questions he didn't seem to expect answers to, all in a hot airless room which was gradually sapping his will. Leric he could understand. He appreciated the relationship between the police and the criminals. If there was something to be said, it was said over a few drinks in a bar, or else in one of those cubbyhole interview rooms where they thought they had the edge because there were half a dozen D's having a go at you.

Leric wiped his forehead with the back of his hand while Harvey wasn't looking. It's getting like a bloody Turkish bath in here, he swore silently. And the interrogation . . . a pro-con couldn't do worse; the sooner Harvey went back to his swede-bashing countryside, the better.

Colin Harvey was well pleased; he had evaluated the change in the two men, the drooping eyelids and the shortening of breath had not passed unnoticed.

'You're in the fruit business, eh, how's it doing?'

Jesus, thought Farrow, what's that supposed to mean? 'I can't grumble.'

'You like this city?'

'It's OK.'

'How about Mace? What do you think about Jack Mace, your partner?'

'What do you mean?'

'Will it affect the business, his bit of trouble?'

'Look, Mace and me was business partners, nothing else. I didn't know anything about that furs job which put him inside. His private life's his own.' Farrow was anxious to keep Mace out of the conversation and the sudden switch in the questioning troubled him.

Harvey leaned back in his chair and folded his arms. It was time.

'Who's putting the squeeze on you, Farrow?'

The question, sharply spoken after the long preamble, caught Farrow off guard. He started in the chair, blinked, then wiped his forehead, too late to hide the reaction his eyes had given away. 'Jesus, it's hot in here,' he managed at last. 'I . . . er didn't catch that last question, Mr Harvey.'

'Someone's putting the arm on you, Farrow, knocking off your lads one at a time. It'll be your turn soon.'

Farrow had recovered his wits. 'You must be joking. I've got no beef with anyone.'

Harvey continued as though he hadn't heard the answer. 'They think that now Mace is out of the way, the field's wide open.' The DI leaned forward across the desk, his eyes fixed on Farrow's face. 'I'll tell you something now, Barney. I'm not interested in you or any of these others.' He tapped a file with his fingers. 'As far as I'm concerned, you can carve each other up, and I'm not losing any sleep over your little protection racket either, because none of your victims has had the guts to put in a complaint.'

The blood pounded at Farrow's temples and he was on his feet, eyebrows furrowed with sudden anger. 'Look, mate, if you're going to start making allegations, perhaps I'd better get a solicitor round here double quick. I'm not standing for any of that . . .'

Harvey turned to Leric. 'Did you hear me make an allegation, Sergeant?' Leric shook his head silently, glancing up from his notes as Harvey went on: 'Sit down, Barney. Stop getting so bloody jumpy. I'm not going to knock you off, I'm trying to do you a favour.'

'We want the Londoners, and we want them before there's a bloody great battle and a few innocent people get hurt,' Harvey said quickly.

Farrow collected his thoughts; he would have to treat this copper with a little more respect. 'I don't know what you're talking about.'

'Come off it, Barney.' Harvey spread his hands on the desk-top, watching Farrow's face intently. 'It's just a matter of time.'

Farrow shook his head. 'You're talking in riddles, squire. No one from the Smoke would be wasting their time up here.' He cursed his own stupidity. He had been taken in by the copper's seemingly stumbling line of questioning and he'd almost given himself away. But it would take more than a few trick questions to catch Barney Farrow.

'You're not fooling anyone here, Farrow,' Harvey replied. 'We've got you and your henchman in the files where they belong. We know all about you and your mates, where you hang out, who you're sleeping with; every time you pick your nose, Farrow, it goes down in the file. And when a job comes up with your trademark on it, we can guarantee to knock you off in a matter of hours, that's how well we know you, Barney.' Harvey paused and waved a hand at the grey steel filing cabinets which stood in the shadows along the wall. 'You're all pigeon-holed neat and tidy, and the first complaint that comes along will put you away.'

Farrow was needled. 'You're all mouth, mate. I've got a legit business and you can't prove different.'

Harvey shrugged. 'We're not interested in you, Barney, not yet. You're doing our job for us. You're more valuable where you are, alone and vulnerable. This London mob don't pull their punches. My bet is they'll croak you sooner or later and all we'll have to do is keep a close tab on you until it happens, and we've got them.'

Farrow scowled. 'You don't scare me, copper. You're talking to the wrong bloke. How many times I got to tell you, I don't know nothing about it.'

Harvey had tired of the cross play, there was nothing more to be had from Barney Farrow. 'Suit yourself, but don't forget I warned you. Your neck's at stake, not mine.'

Farrow rose from his chair. 'If that's all, I'll be on my way.'

'Nobody's stopping you, Barney, but there's one thing I want you to remember. As far as I'm concerned, you're expendable. You're just a cheap villain who's going to get himself knocked off by someone a shade more ruthless. The murder of Barney Farrow will only make a few lines in the newspapers. You almost copped it once before, and I'd say this time it was guaranteed.'

Farrow just stopped himself touching the scar on his neck and turned to where Leric was holding the door. He hesitated for a second, and Harvey thought he saw a flash of fear in the man's eyes. Then he moved to follow the Sergeant out of the police station.

CHAPTER VII

'FIREMAN' BRADY had well earned his reputation. Since they had arrived in the city, he had disposed of four men and maimed two more. To the thick-set Londoner, death was no more than squashing a fly. He was the technician of the trio, adapting and modifying a skill he had learned in the steel mills of the North to his own crime speciality, and now he laughed inwardly when hardened criminals blanched at the sound of his name.

He had come to the city with the enforcers, Sand and Crouper, to crush the leaderless local underworld. They would take over and expand their empire once the opposition had been brushed aside.

Anyone could kill, Brady had decided, the act of murder was an easy thing, a split second and it was all over, but disposing of the body was something much more difficult, something which had tripped many a professional. Brady had solved the problem, and for that one reason he was promoted to the élite of the underworld. He had taken the risk out of killing and had made death a marketable commodity.

Tonight he was angry.

He sat in the back of the van as Crouper drove along the side-streets, his face taut with the rage which welled up inside him. He had tried to explain that what they planned was far too risky with the sort of equipment he was using, but they had been too bone-headed to listen to reason. Well, if it bloody well went wrong, he would make sure that the blame was laid at the right door. Alex Shapiro had no place for bunglers.

Tom, the night-watchman, had finished his round of the warehouse, satisfying himself that everything was in order. He made one last check on the main gates and went back to his office, the light from his torch flashing on the high-piled crates of fruit.

He had feared he would lose his job when Mace was sent to prison, for it had been he who had opened the main doors when the police came with a search warrant. He had tried to protest, but they had brushed him aside and started turning the place over. It had not come as a surprise that Mace was a criminal, for he had turned a blind eye to the strange comings and goings late at night at the warehouse; they were none of his business.

Soon he would be seventy, without hope of finding other work, and he had fretted for a fortnight before plucking up the courage to ask Barney Farrow if he was to be sacked. But to his surprise, Farrow had given him two fivers out of his own pocket and told him to carry on as usual.

Tom climbed the wooden stairs, pulling himself up by the handrail until he was on the boardwalk of the gallery. He shone his torch on the neat stacks of crates below and then opened the door to his office and went inside. Ellen, his daughter, was sitting by the paraffin heater in the corner of the room.

'Everything all right, Dad?' She looked up as he appeared in the doorway.

'Safe and sound,' he replied cheerfully. 'Thanks for bringing the soup, love. I'd forget my head if it wasn't screwed on. You'd best be getting back home, no sense in both of us staying up all night.'

'Oh, a few more minutes won't hurt.'

'All right,' said the old man, 'but not too long, then.'

'It's nice and cosy in here, Dad,' she said, changing the subject. 'I nearly brought your overcoat, it's gone quite nippy tonight.'

Tom walked over to the heater, rubbing his hands. 'I look after meself never fear. I'm warm enough with this heater and there's a drum of paraffin downstairs, so I won't be catching cold . . .'

A noise outside caught the old man's attention and he cocked his head like a dog listening to the night.

'What is it, Dad?'

'Hush up a minute, I can hear summat.'

There it was again, a clang of metal, louder this time, from the direction of the big roller shutter at the front of the warehouse.

'I'd best take a look. You stay here in the warm, Ellen, I won't be a jiffy. It's probably just a rat, but I'll nip down just to be on the safe side.'

Tom closed the door behind him and stepped out on to the boardwalk. He leaned on the balustrade and stared down into the darkness below. The silence was absolute, but his senses were keyed up and all of a sudden the ever-present stench of rotten fruit seemed overpowering. He shuffled towards the staircase when the clatter of something striking the big metal door startled him.

Quickly he snapped on his torch and swung the beam towards the door, hurrying down the stairs as fast as his rheumatic legs would carry him. The torchlight bounced off the metal slats as he almost ran towards the door along the aisle between the stacked crates. The metallic crunch of the bolt-cutter echoed against the high corrugated roof and the big door began to swing upwards.

'Hey! . . . hey, what's goin' on!' The torch-beam jerked as the watchman broke into a shambling run. The door continued to slide up and he caught a glimpse of a dark-ened tailboard of a van reversing into the opening.

Waving his arms excitedly, he shouted, 'Hey—hey, you can't . . .' A hand clamped over his mouth, pinching his nose, and he felt his head begin to spin. His arms were pinned behind him and his creaking muscles could do nothing to break free. As he fought for breath, a harsh voice next to his ear said, 'Take it easy, dad, and you won't get hurt . . .' And then he was falling into the bottomless pit of oblivion.

Crouper leaned out of the side window and began to

reverse the van down the central aisle of the warehouse, cursing as the side crashed into a pile of crates, scattering them in his path.

At the open rear doors, Brady was busy with his equipment, the portable welding torch already alight. He moved the valves on the oxygen bottles and a sheet of white flame roared across the inside of the warehouse, showering a rainfall of sparks on the wooden crates. He made a quick adjustment to control the flame from the confined space in the back of the van. He had told them it couldn't be adapted for something like this, but they wouldn't listen.

High above the warehouse floor, Ellen heard her father's cry and ran out of the watchman's office to see what had happened. From her vantage point on the balcony, she saw his slumped figure being dragged outside and the van reversing into the opening. All her instincts said scream—scream and run. But there was nowhere to run to, except down the stairs the way her father had gone.

She turned back into the office and slammed the door. It would be safe here for the moment, they would not know that she was in the warehouse. They would think the watchman would be alone. She had a few moments. I must get help . . . help. She had looked frantically around the small room before she saw it. The telephone.

Her hand shaking from shock, Ellen picked up the old dusty bakelite handset and tried to keep her finger still enough to dial the three nines. The telephone rang for what seemed like an age, then a disembodied voice said : 'Emergency—which service?'

Her gratitude at the sudden communication with another human being shook everything she had ever remem-

bered about emergency calls out of her head. 'Emergency
—which service, please?' The voice was sharper now.
'Police . . .' she managed at last, hardly recognizing the
hoarse terrified whisper that was her voice. 'Please . . . get
me the police.'

The operator asked for her name and telephone number, and Ellen was trying to focus her spinning mind on
the digits printed on the dial when a flash of light and the
sound of crashing glass startled her so badly that she
dropped the telephone. On her hands and knees on the
floor, she managed to find the instrument in the darkness
which had suddenly invaded the watchman's office.
'Please,' she sobbed into the instrument, beside herself
with panic. 'They've got my father. It's the fruit warehouse in St Martin's Lane . . . the Victoria Storage
Company . . . Please help me.'

In the softly lit telephone exchange, the GPO operator reached across his board to connect the call to the
police central information room and found the line had
gone dead. He began to trace the call from the information scrawled on his pad.

Brady could not control the tongue of flame leaping
from the equipment in his hands. He swore softly as he
struggled to balance the valves, his face livid in the glare
from the sheet of fire which spurted molten crimson
daggers high into the tall roofed building. He had told
them it wouldn't work and he'd been right. It wasn't
meant for this sort of bloody flame-thrower lark. He was
closing the tap of the twin canisters when the explosion
threw him off balance and sent him sprawling inside the
van, the nozzle writhing like a living thing in his slackened
grasp. A dull thud rebounded from the warehouse wall

as the paraffin drum went up in an orange fireball with a shock wave which crumpled the wooden staircase to the balcony. Brady worked feverishly to unscrew the coupling in his asbestos-gauntleted hands and shouted to Crouper in the cab, 'For Christ's sake, get moving!'

He need not have wasted his breath. The driver had seen for himself and was revving the engine. The gears crunched and the van shot out of the warehouse and skidded into the street, as Brady threw the white-hot stub in a long cartwheel out of the vehicle. A shower of sparks smouldered dangerously beside the sprawled figure of the watchman on the pavement outside the warehouse, which was already an inferno of flames.

CHAPTER VIII

ONE THING the villains of London's East End knew for certain about Alex Shapiro; he was at his most dangerous when he smiled.

Shapiro leaned down to the glass-topped coffee table, powerful shoulder-muscles rippling under his tailor-made shirt. A heavy gold signet ring gleamed on the finger of his broad hand as it closed around the whisky bottle. He sat back in the deep armchair and poured himself a drink, half filling the squat tumbler. After loosening the jacket of his hand-stitched suit, he leaned back in the soft leather and swallowed the drink, dropping the tumbler in front of him. He picked up the bottle again, held it up to the light and swirled the whisky until it danced with reflections, then with one smooth movement he hurled the bottle across the room and it shattered on the pine panelling, the amber liquid trickling down the wall and soaking into the deep pile of the fitted carpet. Alex Shapiro was smiling.

'Tell me,' he said almost lazily, 'why was the woman killed?'

Crouper licked his lips with a dry tongue and tried hard to fight back the fear rising in his throat. 'It was a mistake, honest, boss, we never meant to croak her. We didn't even know she was in the bloody warehouse.'

Shapiro ran a hand over the tight black curls of his short hair and glanced at the others, waiting. Sand shrugged and averted his eyes.

Brady met his employer's questioning smile. 'I told 'em it was too risky and it went wrong. But then I don't make the decisions, do I?'

Shapiro turned again to Crouper, the man he had appointed leader of the operation in the city. The man he expected to get things done quickly and without trouble or mess, the man who would carry the can. His voice had the quality of silk. 'We can't afford mistakes, can we, Martin?' Crouper was shocked to hear the use of his first name. He had seen Shapiro's wrath before, and always, always, the victim was addressed by his first name. It struck terror deep into the man, but he knew he dared not show it. A glimpse of weakness and Shapiro would certainly dispose of him like a broken straw.

'Remember Mitchell?' Shapiro went on. 'He made a mistake too, now he's supporting the Chiswick fly-over. Then there was Anton—' he shook his head, frowning slightly at the memory—'he proved unreliable after such good beginnings. I had high hopes of him, as I have for you, Martin. Even the fish didn't fancy him after a taste of the lance, eh? We've got no room for failures in this business. All I ask is a little loyalty—' he tapped a finger to his temple, his eyes never leaving Crouper's—'and a little brains. Now you tell me just what else you've been doing.'

They had returned to London discreetly, leaving the car at Swiss Cottage and crossing the city by tube, watchful that they were not spotted by any of the heavy-mob D's who knew their faces. Now they were back in their own stamping-ground, the back streets of the East End, close to the docks. Shapiro had his headquarters there, safe, among his own kind.

'We've got 'em beat hands down, Mr Shapiro.' Crouper desperately needed to impress his boss. 'All the local strong-arm guys have been taken care of and there's only Farrow left. That was what the fire was all about. We reckon he'll throw his hand in now; half his lads have changed sides already, they don't want any bother. We're set up in a garage owned by a geezer named Spauling, it's a perfect cover. He's in hospital after a little accident.' He waited for a reaction, but Shapiro was still relaxed in the chair, his eyes closed. 'We've moved the croupiers into the clubs, a few at a time. You just say the word, boss, and we'll move in on the Mace operation.'

Shapiro opened one eye a fraction. 'Tell me about the transport.'

Crouper licked his lips again. 'We've got a dozen motors on tap,' he replied. 'We put the arm on a couple of other motor-dealers and now we've got all the transport we need, Mr Shapiro.'

'What's the take look like?'

'Upwards of ten grand a week with the clubs. It'll be like shelling peas. Mace only scratched the surface.'

'How about the law? You had any bother with the D's?'

Crouper forced a laugh. 'They're a bunch of hayseeds compared with our lot. We left a motor for them to watch and they've been sitting there like clay pigeons ever since. The law ain't sussed a thing, Mr Shapiro, and the local villains know better than to go rabbitting to the coppers after the medicine we've been handing out.'

Shapiro jerked upright, his face snapping taut like a trap and his black eyes burning with a sudden ferocity. His voice was harsh as steel on a grindstone. 'You'd better be right, my son, because an old friend at the Yard is taking an unhealthy interest in our operation here. Frenchie the Fixer from the Flying Squad, only now he's got himself a big number with the Yard and he's anxious to make an impression. Well, it's not going to be with my neck. You seen any of the Yard blokes at your end?'

Crouper swallowed the lump in his throat. 'We been too careful, boss. Like I said, the law ain't got a smell of us. We had a couple of tails up the motorway early on, but you know all about those. Since we gave them the slip, we ain't seen any law at all, straight up.'

Shapiro nodded his carefully barbered head. 'I believe you, Martin. Only now this woman's been killed, the local law's going to get all excited. Maybe it's time we paid a few of them off before they cramp our style. You think about that.' He glanced at the others again. 'You've been saying "we" a lot of times, Crouper, but I ain't heard a peep out of these two brass monkeys. They lost their tongues or something? Brady—how about you? What do you think about the set-up?'

'It stinks,' said Brady shortly, glad of the chance to halt

Crouper's attempts to crawl out of his own private cess-
pit. 'This Farrow's a tough nut, he ain't going to crack
just like that. Now this woman's croaked, he's going to go
running to the law, because if he don't, he's the number
one suss and I can't see him standing still for that one.
With Mace inside and his outfit all cracked up, he's got
nothing to lose. I reckon we should have done a deal with
him before, but like I say, I just take orders.'

Shapiro watched their faces, blank, expressionless, offering no emotion, the faces of professional criminals hardened by hours of police interrogation. He would use them
while they had something to offer, until he had squeezed
the last drop of criminal talent from them, until they were
no longer an investment. Shapiro concentrated on the
present, invested for the future, and wrote his own history
under the title of self-preservation.

'All right,' he said at length, folding his arms across his
deep chest. 'Killing the woman was a big blunder, but I'm
going to wait and see what happens before any decisions
are made. If we have to pull out after all the hard work
I've put into setting up this operation, then somebody's
going to find himself carrying a white stick and selling
matches on Hyde Park Corner, and that's if he's lucky.'
Shapiro rose. 'You get back up there and straighten things
out. I want results and I want them fast.'

As he left the office, Brady decided to keep one thing to
himself, something which if discovered by Shapiro would
sign their death warrants as surely as if they had made
written confessions to the police. Something had been left
behind at the warehouse fire, and as far as Brady was
concerned, he might just as well have dropped a visiting
card.

CHAPTER IX

THEY WERE WASTING their time with the old man, Leric
decided. He could tell them nothing, certainly not now,
perhaps not ever. The blow on the watchman's head
had left the right side of his body paralysed, and he
lay propped up in the hospital bed, one side of his face
a bland mask, while the other, lips, nostril and eyebrow,
twitched uncontrollably from the delayed shock.

Leric looked down at the old man, conscious of
Veitch standing beside him, the case containing the
Identikit slides and the CRO pictures, hanging loosely
in the detective's hand. Poor old sod, thought Leric with
unaccustomed compassion. You should have been propping your slippers on the fireplace instead of sitting
around a draughty warehouse all night for a few lousy
quid. Look what it's got you, dad; you'll maybe never
walk again, or think a constructive thought. Better that
way, perhaps, better you shouldn't know how she died.

'She was his only child,' said Leric, thinking his
thoughts out loud. 'No other relatives.'

Veitch nodded. 'Why'd they want to cripple an old
man, Sarge?'

'He got in their way, that's why, son.' Leric pushed
his hands deep into his mackintosh pockets. 'It's as
simple as that. And I don't suppose they even bothered
to find out if there was anybody else in the place before
they started the fire.'

'Our mob, is it?'

'Sticks out like a sore thumb. It's their MO. They've

got a fancy for burning and by the time this is over, they'll be burning themselves, in the fires of hell.'

The sergeant turned and sniffed the ether-laden air, reflecting that he was spending too much time in hospitals on this job. 'You stick with him and if he says anything that makes sense, get it in your book.' He looked down at the bed again, 'Only I think you're going to have a long wait. I'll have you relieved at lunch-time.'

Leric left Veitch at the hospital and drove across the city to the warehouse. The twisted roof girders poked blackened fingers at the sky, and firemen in soiled tunics were sloshing about in the charred sodden debris, damping down the small pockets of smouldering embers. A stench of burnt fruit cloyed the warm air, and the detective fought back a spasm of nausea as he walked towards the knot of men standing near the gateway. He picked his way across the tangle of high-pressure hoses, past the parked fire-engines, their blue beacons revolving lazily to the crackle of messages from the cab radios. He saw the distinctive white helmet of the Divisional Fire Officer and recognized the others as a detective-constable from the division and a couple of plainclothes men from the coroner's office.

The DO detached himself from the group and walked over to meet him, his face soot-stained and his eyes squinting red-rimmed from the effects of the smoke. The grey grime-encrusted stubble on the fire officer's chin told its own story of a long hard night directing the fire-fighting operations. Despite his obvious fatigue, the DO managed a smile.

'You're a bit late, Sergeant, your lads have gone.'

Leric returned the smile. He had plenty of time for

firemen; their job was one step worse than a copper's, all risk and very little reward.

'I called in at the hospital to see the old chap. He's in a bad way.'

'Can't be worse than the daughter. They've got what's left of her down at the mortuary.'

Leric met the fireman's eyes. 'Where did you find her?'

The DO pointed a bloody, grazed hand at the inside of the blackened shell. 'We got inside under the water jets with BA sets . . . it was like opening a furnace door. She was up in the office—dead, when we found her. The smoke got to her before we did. We were bringing her out when the staircase collapsed.' The fireman looked at his hand, observing the blood still oozing from between the knuckles, as if for the first time. 'Two of the lads are in hospital, the burning timbers caught them.' He shook his head. 'You'd better get the bastards who started this little lot. They ought to be topped.'

'Deliberate, then, you reckon?' Leric watched the fireman's face, set hard beneath the grime. 'Any ideas how it started?'

'It's an oxygen fire. Saw plenty of them in the war. When there's enough oxygen in a confined space, it all goes up with one almighty bang.' The DO pointed at the girders. 'They tell their own story, coated with oxide.'

Leric frowned. 'You mean the place was full of oxygen when it went up?'

'That's exactly what I mean. It sticks out a mile if you know anything about fires. There's no seat to be found, no slow-smouldering flame-spread or flash-point, it went up all in one go.'

'Arson?' asked Leric.

'Only one way I know that oxygen could have got in there in enough quantity for the place to go up as quick as it did—it was pumped in. No question about it.'

Leric watched a team of firemen dragging a hose-reel through the charred woodwork, sparks showering around their heavy boots. Wisps of black smoke still hung in the air. 'What do you think?' he asked at last.

The fireman wiped his hand across his sweaty forehead, leaving behind a bloody smear. 'You'd better ask your chief. Some blokes from the Forensic came down and took away a few bits and pieces. If you want my guess, I'd say someone's made himself a flame-thrower.'

Flame-thrower—the words triggered a switch in the detective's brain. Eddie Roach's hand was burned off, so the whisper went; Ted Spauling too, they found him with his body a mass of burns. How many more they hadn't heard about? And this was Barney Farrow's warehouse, Farrow who was the last corner of resistance against the London mob. If they had a flame-thrower, it would explain a lot of things.

Leric gripped the DO's shoulder. 'I'll remember you when we get 'em, sir, and if I was you, I'd have that hand seen to. It looks a bit nasty.'

He walked back to his car, thankful that the job of sifting through the evil-smelling wreckage of the warehouse was in other hands, and headed back to the police station.

CHAPTER X

ANDERSON WAS a Doctor of Physics and Director of the Regional Forensic Science Laboratory. He was also a past master at breaking down the technical jargon of the scientists into terms which even a layman could understand.

He glanced over his spectacles at the policemen, waiting until he had their attention. They were standing around a white Formica-topped exhibits' table in the laboratory: Harvey and Leric from the Regional Squad, the Coroner's Chief Inspector and a divisional detective-constable.

'If you're quite ready, gentlemen.' Anderson stilled the hum of conversation with a sharp glance. He beckoned to a white-coated assistant, who handed him a polythene bag which had been tagged with an exhibit label. Anderson opened the bag on the table and a blackened metal tube, about three feet long, rolled on to the Formica.

The scientist tapped it with his pencil. 'Exhibit A,' he read from the label, 'section of piping recovered from the roadway outside the Victoria Storage Company warehouse, St Martin's Lane, 02.38 hours today.' Anderson looked up from the scrawled label. 'Bright lad, the copper who found this,' he said, rubbing his hands. 'A very interesting piece of evidence indeed. Anybody got any ideas what it is?'

The DC from the division fell for it, and became the butt for a little of Anderson's dry humour. 'The weapon used to club the watchman, sir?' he asked eagerly.

Anderson clucked his tongue. 'I said interesting, son. When was a bloody cosh interesting . . .' He glanced around the faces, but none of the others had anything to offer.

'No,' he said at length, pausing for effect, 'not a cosh, gentlemen. If you look at it a bit closer, you will see it's a three-eighths of an inch steel tube packed with mild steel rods. It's exactly thirty-four and a half inches long and one end's threaded.' He paused. 'Anybody else want to do my job for me?' The DC flushed as Anderson eyed the policemen. No one spoke. 'Well, then,' he went on, 'I'll tell you: it's the stub of a thermic lance.'

Leric caught his breath. The scientist's words had been like a physical blow. Leric had heard of thermic lances, of course, they had been used a few times down in the Smoke mainly, on bank jobs, some sort of cutting gear, but he had never taken any particular interest in them. They were too specialized for the villains of this city. Plastic gelly was still good enough for the local petermen. He saw the same puzzlement on Harvey's face. The implications seemed to have gone over the heads of the other two policemen; they stood expressionless as if waiting for a foreign word to be translated.

Anderson watched, mildly amused. He should have known that the technical niceties of civil engineering would be wasted. 'For those of us present,' he began, glancing pointedly at the DC from the division who was trying to hide his discomfort with an intelligent smile, 'who may not be too well up on the techniques of thermic boring, we'd better begin with a little explanation, because someone in this city is very well versed in lancing operations.'

He picked up the piece of tubing and weighed it in

his hands. 'The system was developed at the end of the last war, principally for cutting through large concrete structures, and was first employed in the demolition of submarine pens and gun emplacements. The process is simple enough. Oxygen is fed through a length of steel gas barrel packed with mild steel rods which is held by a lance-holder, an adaptor fitted with a valve and connected to an oxygen supply. A standard lance is ten feet long, and the oxygen is passed through the tube where it reacts with the iron in the rods; then the lance is ignited by a blow-pipe flame held to the tip until the ignition temperature is reached, triggering an iron-oxidizing reaction which produces intense heat.' He paused again and turned the lance stub in his hands, inspecting the heat-seared metal. 'In fact the reaction is sufficient to melt concrete at a temperature of between 1,800 and 2,500 degrees centigrade. The lance is screwed into the holder by the threaded end so that it can easily be replaced when it has burned down as short as this one has, and the usual source of oxygen supply is from small cylinders of somewhere near 240 cubic feet capacity, which makes it quite portable. In the hands of an experienced operator, a thermic lance can be used to slice through reinforced concrete as if it were butter. This aspect of the lancing development did not escape the more imaginative of the criminal community, and as you know, lances have been used to pierce the vaults of banks and other strong-rooms in a number of robberies.' He placed the lance stub back on the table and looked up at the officers. 'It looks as if some bright monkey has found yet another use for it.'

Colin Harvey cleared his throat. 'Wasn't there a serial

number system introduced to keep a check on all the lances in circulation, so that if one went missing it could easily be traced?' Harvey's scant information came from a Metropolitan police notification he recalled seeing some time ago.

Anderson nodded. 'Yes, Inspector, every lance manufactured is stamped with a special serial number to try and prevent them falling into the wrong hands. I've not been able to find one on this stub, even under the microscope, so I can only conclude that someone outside the law made it. The rest will be up to you.'

The coroner's officer was clearly confused, but he felt obliged to add something to the discussion. 'I wonder if you could let me have a full report in writing, sir,' he said with dull tenacity, 'for the Coroner, you understand. This may have some relevance at the inquest.' He couldn't for the life of him see what relevance a piece of pipe used for cutting concrete could have in the death of the woman in the warehouse blaze, but if Anderson thought it important, then it must be.

Harvey hoped to take it a stage further. 'In your opinion, Doctor,' he asked slowly, 'could this lance have been used to start the warehouse fire?'

Anderson shrugged. 'You'd need an expert in pyrotechnics to answer that one for sure. I'd say it could have, if the lance tip was brought up to operational heat and then the oxygen pressure suddenly stepped up. It would produce the twofold effect of impregnating the air inside the warehouse with oxygen and shooting out a shower of white-hot iron oxide slag which would set fire to anything it landed on.'

Harvey nodded. 'How could we find out for sure—what would be the evidence?'

Anderson picked up the lance stub. 'This is a good start. Then there's bound to be some oxidization inside the building and slag too, but all that's probably been buried under the debris from the fire. There are no fingerprints on this, and I wouldn't have expected any. For a start, it was exposed to the fire, and if the assumption that an operator started the blaze with the lance is right, he had to unscrew this stub in a hurry. It would have been too hot to handle with bare hands, and if he's as experienced as he seems to be, he would have been wearing asbestos gloves. I'd say you want to find the rest of the equipment, the lance-holder and the oxygen cylinders. We may be able to get some comparison tests done then, but first you've got to find them, Mr Harvey.' The scientist smiled suddenly. 'Even then it'd never stand up in court by itself.' He slipped the lance stub back into its polythene cover and faced the policemen. 'I'll tell you another thing about thermic lances, lads,' he said quietly. 'I saw one in operation a couple of years ago on a Home Office course. There's a white-hot flame, showers of sparks and smoke and its stuck in my mind: it doesn't make a sound. All that power and no noise at all.' The scientist sought about for a word outside the technical books which would sum up what he wanted to convey. 'Uncanny,' he said at last, 'that's what it was. Uncanny.'

Landon was waiting for them in the crime squad office, a cold smile on his mouth.

'You can forget the silent service caper now, lads. We're going to have a crack at it now.' He tapped his chest with a forefinger.

Harvey knew he was right. The death of the woman

had shifted the emphasis of the inquiry. It was a city crime, committed within the area of the city force, and theirs to claim by right. There would be no more liaison with the Regional Squad, they would be called in to assist if necessary, but Harvey doubted whether their help would be asked for. The woman's death and the implications it brought had changed things, and there were reputations at stake.

Landon jerked his thumb at the open doorway. 'Your gaffer's in with the Chief now, getting the worst end of it I wouldn't doubt. The Chief's an old-fashioned copper, he doesn't hold with this watch-and-wait routine. Still, you can leave the grafting to us now, can't you, lads?'

Harvey let the jibe ride, there was no point in antagonizing a senior detective of the local force. You had to be a bloody politician on this job.

Landon glanced at Leric, delighted at the tightening of the detective's lips. 'You should know better, Sergeant. Didn't I teach you anything on the city squad? Knock 'em off when you can, lad, and leave the fancy footwork to the college-boy coppers down the Met, it's about their bottle.'

'You've got some ideas, sir?' Harvey asked as pleasantly as he could.

Landon grinned. 'Every copper's got ideas, son, it's making 'em work that counts. First off, we're going to turn over Barney Farrow. This little lot was intended to teach him a lesson and he'll know who's dishing out the punishment. I'll be interested to know where he was last night when the fire started.'

Harvey reached across his desk and opened the inquiry file, leafing through the carefully indexed statements. 'I don't think you'll have any bother there, Mr Landon.

He was right here in this office with Leric and me.'
He extracted a carbon copy of a closely typed statement
and handed it to Landon. 'Here's a transcript of our interview with him. It's full of nothing.'

Landon glanced down the foolscap sheet in an effort
to hide his displeasure. 'All the same,' he replied, 'we'll
have him in again just in case he's remembered anything since.' He turned towards the door.

'How about the newspapers, sir?' Harvey asked quickly.
The fire had already attracted considerable interest.

Landon shook his head briefly. 'On a job like this,
I treat the Press like mushrooms. Keep 'em in the dark
and feed 'em on bullshit.' He winked and disappeared
into the corridor.

Leric felt a curious resentment which he could not
put his finger on; he had joined the Regional Squad from
the city force full of reservations about the new aspect
of the job, that of concentrating on the criminals rather
than the crime, but already he could feel an identification with the work and suddenly the old sledge-hammer
tactics seemed unfamiliar.

'Don't worry about Harry,' he said to Harvey as the
DI slipped the folder back into his desk, 'he's all chat.
The only way he ever lifted anyone was by having him
brought in on a plate. How do you think he got his nickname?' All the same, it grieved Leric to see the squad
standing down on what had been their inquiry.

Landon and his team questioned Farrow for most of
the afternoon in the central CID. They intercepted
him when he went to see the ruins of his business for
himself, and took him to the police-station.

Two floors above the interrogation room where the

shirt-sleeved detectives were bombarding Farrow with
questions about the fire, Colin Harvey sat at his desk
and turned the new developments over in his mind. He
had been called in to Strickland's room soon after the
Co-ordinator had returned from his meeting with the
Chief Constable, and had been told that their operation
was to be changed.

He recalled Strickland's words: 'These are bad
bastards, Harvey. We're going to have to put the gipsy's
warning on them before more innocent people get involved. Never mind Landon and his lads, we're going to
put the squeeze on this mob before it's too late. I'll
telex French and put him in the picture.'

Harvey mulled it over slowly. They were smart operators, the Londoners, and they'd gone to ground somewhere in the city without even a smell. It would take
some doing, flushing them out; they'd need a copper on
every street corner.

The telephone rang. It was the outside line and
Harvey answered with just the exchange and number.
The caller was the detective-constable on duty at the
hospital.

'When did he die?' Harvey asked quickly. Half an
hour ago. He looked at his watch, planning the next
move. 'All right. Get them to move the body over to the
central mortuary. I'll fix up a priority release and square
it with the coroner.' This could be the break, Harvey
decided. Played right, it could be the break they had
been waiting for. He made two quick calls on the
internal telephone, the second confirming that Farrow
was still in the building.

Barney Farrow gave them nothing. It was the same old

routine, the blustering, the table-thumping and the threats. He was used to it. A bunch of stupid coppers busting a gut with the same old moody he'd heard a thousand times before. He told Landon nothing and he smiled as he did so. After three hours in the interrogation room, they let Farrow go.

He walked across the police station yard to his parked Jaguar and was bending, key in hand, at the driver's door when a shadow fell on the gleaming bodywork. Colin Harvey leaned on the car door and squinted in the watery sunlight as Farrow straightened. Harvey's first impression was that Farrow looked drawn, his eyes had sunk deeper behind the heavy brows and glowed like hot coals.

'Spare me a minute, Barney. There's something I want you to see.' Harvey smiled.

Farrow hunched his shoulders. 'I've had a bellyful of coppers for one day. Can't you leave it, I'm a busy man?'

Harvey ran a hand across the roof of the car. 'I wouldn't ask if it wasn't important, and it'll only take a minute. You'll be interested. I'll guarantee that.'

Farrow's face closed in a black scowl. What did this country copper want now? Another boy-scout lecture? He looked around the car park, anxious to leave this place which stank of the enemy, anxious to get the law off his back. If he didn't do what this bugger asked, they'd only bring him in again when it suited them, when he didn't have a choice. He would let them play their games this time, they had nothing on him.

'OK, squire,' said Farrow in a tired voice. ' 'Ave it your way, then.' He stepped away from the car.

'That's right, Barney,' Harvey replied. 'Make it easy on yourself. We don't want any hard feelings, do we?'

He led the way across the road to the red brick court building next door to the science laboratory. They went through the open swing-doors into the cool interior and Harvey guided Farrow along a corridor which smelt of sweat and polish, past a notice board marked Coroner's Court and down a flight of steps into the basement. He paused at a low green door, pulled it open and ushered Farrow inside.

The long room in which he was standing was in shadow, a chill rising from the stone floor in sharp contrast with the warm sunshine outside. Farrow thought they must be somewhere in the basement, and the cold draught numbed his ankles. He wrinkled his nose, trying to place the sweet smell of chemicals mixed with something else . . . something he couldn't put his finger on, but which left a clammy sensation in the small of his back.

Harvey clicked on the light and the room took shape : white windowless walls, a glass-topped table on heavy iron legs, and along the length of one side of the room, a row of locker boxes with typed cards in the metal holders. Farrow felt an awful dread creep over him. He felt a compelling desire to get out of this place before anything else happened. The odour he recognized now, for it was like no other. It was the smell of death. A little ferret of a man pulling on a stained white coat came scurrying towards them. Farrow swallowed hard, and heard Harvey speaking.

'Never seen a mortuary before, Barney? Never mind, it smells worse than it is, eh, Charlie?'

The little man grinned broken teeth. 'I was told to

expect you, Mr Harvey. We just put him in number four. I ain't had time to make out a card yet, 'im 'avin' passed away so recent, like.'

The attendant led the way across to the bank of lockers, which Farrow realized were the refrigerated resting-places of the corpses. He was aware of Harvey's hand on his elbow.

'What's the game, then? Why you brought me in 'ere?' Farrow tried to keep his voice from quavering.

'Just something you ought to see, old son,' Harvey insisted, drawing him closer to the grey fronts of the lockers.

Barney's head was beginning to swim and the chill gripped him now, cold sweat standing on his forehead. Charlie's smile wavered in front of his eyes.

Harvey reached forward in what seemed slow motion and pulled the handle on a drawer. It slid out on oiled rollers as Farrow watched, horrified. Go on, you bastard, have a look, have a bloody good look. Harvey gripped Farrow's arm and pushed him forward. The face of the dead man was a waxen mask, eyes still open but clouded with the opaque film of dying, the torso scarred with dull weals, and puckered blind mouths gaped where the drip-feeds had entered. The singed hair on the belly and groin was shaved in patches and the skin lacerated from the surgeon's knife; the legs were limp and the colour of kneaded dough. A brown card tag was tied loosely to the right big toe.

Harvey reached down and flipped it over with his forefinger. 'Your mate Ted Spauling, Barney. Died this afternoon from bronchial pneumonia. Have a close look, he didn't go easy.'

Farrow gagged, his mind a blank as the waves of

horror swept over him. He lurched sideways and gave way to the nausea, vomiting on the clean floor. Harvey was supporting his weight, speaking slowly so that every word sank in.

'Remember what I told you, Farrow, I'm waiting for that call. You're next. Be warned.'

Barney Farrow drove his Jaguar like an automaton. He desperately needed to clear his mind so that he could think and plan again, but the picture of the thing in the mortuary, the tortured grisly corpse of his friend, flooded back, stubbornly resisting his conscious will.

Ted had died in a torment of pain, that much was obvious. How had it happened? Farrow concentrated all his efforts to push the question away and lost the battle. Had he known he was going to die from the moment the two men called for him at his home? Was there something in their hard eyes which had spelled out death, or did it take him by surprise, a tap on the head and then the flame? Was that how it had been? Farrow shuddered; it would be indescribable terror and then just a void of blind pain with the burning. The copper was right, he thought bitterly, they're saving me for something special. This whole thing's been played out for my benefit to show me how ruthless these fingers are, and now I'm the only mug left on their list. The fire at the warehouse had shaken him badly and now Spauling had croaked . . . Would he be the next victim?

How would it come? He tried to stop the fantasies. Like Eddie; would it be like that? A quick neat burning job and just a blackened stump for a hand to prove he was a mug. No. Eddie had been the first, he had been a walking, snivelling, sobbing warning that this mob meant business. He remembered how Miller had stood ashen-faced at the door of his flat. He had walked out to the car and looked at the writhing form in the back seat, moaning like an animal in agony. They had had to move quickly to get Eddie out of the city to a shady nursing-home they had used many times before. A place where no questions were asked. God, thought Farrow, that seemed like an age ago. No, it wouldn't be like Eddie, or any of the others. He would be finished, there was no reason to cripple him, to maim or disfigure. He was the last one left, there were no more warnings necessary, no more grisly reminders and no one left to impress. Farrow wiped the back of his hand across his forehead and was surprised to feel the chill of cold sweat still there. For an instant, he felt safe in the car, cut off and remote by virtue of the 50 m.p.h. on the speedometer.

What if he just kept on driving, turned his back on the city and left it all behind? They wouldn't come looking for him, they would have what they wanted. It was tempting, but he would need funds and they were all tied up in the city. Mace, he knew, would never give up, he had the contacts to call in support from outside, resources to take on the London mob on their own terms, and he had never been afraid of a bundle with anybody. He had fought for what was his, had taken from anybody weaker, and had built up his empire on a creed of violence. He had never baulked at doing his own dirty work, either. If trouble arose, he would be there, an iron bar or smashed bottle in his hand. Mace was respected, hated, feared, but . . .

G

Mace was in prison, and this time Barney Farrow had to work out his own salvation.

He let the Jaguar cruise softly, just inside the speed limit, through the thinning traffic on the outskirts of the city. Then there was the law breathing down his neck. Even if he could get a few strong-arm merchants to put up a show when the time came, the law would be watching him and he would stand a more than even chance of going down the steps, if not the hospital. That new copper, Harvey, he knows the score; he knows they'll find me soon, bleeding my guts out in an alley, or worse . . . Perhaps it would work if I just pick up the 'phone like he said . . .

Farrow drove aimlessly for half an hour, his mind in a turmoil. Then he made his decision.

CHAPTER XI

A HEAVY WARM DRIZZLE had fallen that morning, leaving the tall buildings just grey shadows behind the rain curtain. Brady leaned on the window-sill and looked down into the street below. The wet concrete stared back, unmoved.

'Jumpy, aren't you, son.' Crouper was slouched in a chair in the office above Spauling's motor showroom, a half-filled glass in his hand. 'Have a drink.'

Brady turned from the window and picked up one of the morning papers which were scattered about the room. He read the report of the warehouse fire again, searching for a hidden trap in the lines of print, but there was nothing. The story said the police were investigating the possibility of an electrical fault in the building. There was no mention of the discovery of the lance stub.

Crouper picked up the whisky bottle, poured into a tumbler and handed it to Brady, smiling. 'Relax, we'll put the arm on Farrow and all our worries will be over. We can move the boys in and start collecting any time we want to.'

Brady swallowed the drink and waited for the fiery spirit to reach his stomach. He felt the jolt of the whisky deep down in his belly, a warm relaxing glow. He poured another and knocked it back, the reaction stinging the back of his eyes. He felt better. It looked as if the law wouldn't catch on after all, he thought, and now that he'd considered it dispassionately, there was no reason why they should.

A piece of sooty gas pipe, that's all it would look like to them, and such an object found in the debris of a fire wouldn't arouse much interest unless someone recognized its deadly purpose. And what would coppers up here know about thermic lances? Not much. He had considered getting rid of the lance, sending it back to London, somewhere safe, but that would need explanation and Shapiro wasn't a mug. He would have a hard time talking that one away. Instead, Brady had driven the van into the motor workshops at the back of Spauling's garage and had stacked the cylinders and the lance-holder with the welding and cutting equipment in the bodyshop. To the casual eye, it was all the same gear.

'You got some ideas about Farrow, then?' He held the empty glass in his hand and looked down at Crouper. You stupid bastard, he thought, I'd mark you with this if we didn't need you to finish the job. Nobody risks my neck and gets away with it.

Crouper was still smiling. 'Rough him up a little, and if he doesn't want to get out while he's got a chance, maybe we'll croak him like the others . . .'

'No.' Brady was surprised at the sudden sharpness of his own voice. He felt his face drain with anger and the skin pull taut along his jaw. 'Leave off the violence. For Christ's sake, we nearly got blagged the last time.'

Crouper recognized the dangerous edge in the other man's voice. Just as Brady couldn't afford to vent his feelings, Crouper knew he had to keep the 'Fireman' sweet. They were of the same fraternity.

'Me and Sand'll look after old Barney, there's nothing for you to worry about.'

Brady leaned over the man in the chair. 'It's time you learned your lesson, mate. We've got some law in on this caper now, they'll be watching Farrow like hawks and if he gets knocked off, what do you think our chances are then? It's not on any more.'

Crouper helped himself to another drink. 'Blimey, I thought I'd never see the day Fireman Brady went soft.'

Brady moved quickly, and an iron hard forearm locked across Crouper's throat before he could blink. Brady's voice was little more than the hiss of escaping breath. 'You call me soft, sonny, and I'll snap your neck and give you a dose of the lance. It'd be a pleasure to scatter your ashes down the sewer where they belong.'

Crouper swallowed on the bitter bile in his throat. He had seen Brady work, coldly, efficiently. The first man they had killed by mistake when Sand hit him too hard and found he had a weak skull. They'd taken the body round to the scrapyard and Brady had burnt it to a cinder with the white-hot lance flame. The other had been croaked in self-defence. He had been one of the strong-arm men they'd brought in for a bit of a working over. Only when they moved in on him, he'd pulled a machete out of his shirt unexpectedly and swung it at Sand. He was a big man and they'd been taken by surprise, but Crouper had reacted by reflex and used the chiv he always carried up his sleeve. The geezer had dropped, stabbed in the nape of the neck, and Brady had disposed of his body in the same way. Crouper had seen the flame reduce flesh and bone to dust in a matter of seconds. Fear rattled in his throat.

'Come off it,' he whined, badly shaken. 'I was just kiddin' . . . no offence.'

Brady relaxed his grip slowly. 'All right then, but remember, I'd be doing you a favour if you put Shapiro on the spot; he'd have you done soon as look at you.'

Crouper reached for the whisky and poured himself another big drink to steady his nerves. 'Jesus,' he said rubbing his throat, 'I thought you meant to finish me for a second there.'

Brady had stepped back. 'No,' he replied, 'we're still a team, that's the way Shapiro wants it, and he's calling the tune. We just don't take any more risks like that fire fiasco. This time you'll do what I say, we'll talk to Farrow and offer him a deal. If he don't want to know, then we'll fix him, but not before, got it?'

Crouper nodded painfully. 'All right, we'll try it your way, but if he won't have it, you'll burn him just the same.'

'He'll have it, he's got no option,' said Brady softly. 'Now fix up a meet and let's get it over with. I just want my pay-off.' Above all else, Brady was anxious to get back to London, to the comparative safety of the Smoke, and leave the operation in the city to the anonymous collectors who would follow once the set-up was established.

It was early evening on that fickle spring day when Harvey and Leric left the police station, their mac collars turned up against the showers, and collected the Sergeant's car for the half-hour drive out of the city.

The monotonous rhythm of the windscreen-wipers punctuated Harvey's account of the visit to the mortuary, and for the rest of the journey the two detectives sat in silence, staring out at the grey streets, engrossed in their own thoughts.

Harvey had pulled a neat stroke, Leric had to admit that much. He could imagine Farrow's face when the body had slid out in front of his eyes. Leric had seen scores of corpses in various states of mutilation during his CID service, but the act of sudden death never failed to send a sick shudder through him. To someone who had not the same insight into the frailty of the human body, the effect must have been staggering. Harvey was proving to be a right cunning bastard, no doubt about that.

They left the dismal blocks of offices and factories behind as the pavements appeared in front of rows of neat semis, and then came the roadside verges which widened into the landscaped greenery of the more exclusive suburbs. Leric turned off the main road and began to take notice of the wrought-iron gateposts standing sentinel at the end of the in-out drives of the detached homes. He had not been this way for some time, but he knew he would recognize the house when he saw it again. Ted Spauling had graduated to expensive tastes.

The house was easy to recognize, set back behind a sculptured hedge and approached by a sweeping gravel drive to the massive Cotswold stone archway over the front door. The tyres crunched on the loose surface as Leric manœuvred the car through the gateway and stopped in front of the house.

Harvey was out and ringing the doorbell when Leric caught up with him, raindrops glistening in his close-cropped hair. He could see a figure walking along the hallway, distorted by the ripple glass, and then the ornate door opened and Irene Spauling snapped into focus.

She stood in the raised porch looking down at them, her silver-shot hair hanging loose on her shoulders and her mouth set in a bloodless line. She wore no make-up and her eyes were shrouded with a dull sheen which spelt grief beyond tears. She knows, Leric realized at once; she is aware of the fact that her husband is dead, not informed by a telephone voice from the hospital, for the regulations insisted that next of kin be told in person, but by the curious process of osmosis which existed in the criminal classes and which made such things common knowledge the instant they happened.

Harvey must have realized too. 'Can we come inside,' he asked gently, stepping inside the porch, and the woman moved aside in wordless acquiescence.

The detectives followed her along the pine-panelled hall into the lounge, which reflected Spauling's sudden rise to wealth overlaying the inescapable concepts of the back street terraces where the motor-trader's career had begun.

The heavy embossed wallpaper and deep maroon

velvet curtains overpowered the imitation Chinese carpet with its muted colours struggling for survival against the deep-seated black hide settee and easy-chairs. Wall plaques added to the display of tasteless expense, and a lavish cocktail cabinet twinkled a galaxy of cut-glass stars under a plastic imitation of a lily pool housing an electric fountain.

The french door was open and Irene Spauling crossed the room and gazed out at the expanse of lawn as Harvey and Leric waited for her reaction.

Harvey cleared his throat, uncomfortable in the task he had to perform. 'The doctors did all they could,' he began, watching the woman, trying to gauge his approach.

She turned slowly, seeing the two men as if for the first time, immaculate in a pale blue two-piece of light-weight jersey, the jacket falling open to reveal a navy blue blouse. She touched her silver hair in an absent-minded gesture, and the fact that she had obviously not bothered beyond a perfunctory brushing gave the only clue to her knowledge. 'If you've come to tell me Ted's dead, don't bother.' The voice was hard, controlled, and the woman dropped her hand to her left breast, the crimson-varnished nails catching in the fine nylon. 'I know it here . . .'

Leric watched the pale composed face, carefully seeking some hint of weakness, the puffiness which comes from tears. There was none. Of course she would know, he reasoned, she was one of the fraternity wives, one of the women who would not hesitate to go on the game and sell their bodies if necessary, while their menfolk did their time in prison. The men did their bird, kept their mouths shut and their minds closed and talked of trivia when the women came visiting. Only mugs gave trouble, the real professionals just waited for their release day and the next job. Their women waited with them, and so a bond was established far beyond the normal relationship. Irene Spauling had lived long years by the code, accepted from her marriage day and obeyed unswervingly. She would know by instinct her husband was dead.

'It was the shock,' said Harvey, still standing ill at ease. 'The doctors thought he was over the hill, but pneumonia set in and he couldn't fight it.' She nodded briefly and sank into one of the chairs as if unwilling to trust the support of her legs. 'Everyone thought he'd pull through. He was a tough man, but . . .' Harvey tailed off lamely.

'He's dead, isn't he?' Her matter-of-fact tone did not waver. 'Nothing will change that. All right, so he wasn't a lily, granted, but he always treated me right.' The code, thought Leric, as he watched Irene Spauling cross her legs, you'll not be forgetting the code now, Irene. 'Those murdering bastards put an end to him and if I was a man, I'd see to them myself.'

Leric watched the woman's face and saw the flash of anger in her eyes. Will she give in to it, he wondered, will her husband's death end the bond? It wouldn't do to hurry her now. She was looking at them, her body held tight and her hands clasped in her lap; for a second she was all woman as she half-whispered : 'I loved you, Ted, I really did . . .' Then Irene Spauling took a single deep breath. 'Those pictures,' she said finally, her face composed again and just a hint of bitterness creeping into her voice. 'The men who took Ted away were in those pictures you showed me. I don't know their names and I'd never seen them before, but I'll always remember their faces.'

Leric spoke quickly, afraid that Harvey might not grasp what was happening, the revenge struggle which had forced the woman to put aside the criminal code. 'Can I use your phone, Irene? We'd like you to have another look. I'll have them brought over.'

She nodded briefly, dropping her eyes long enough for Leric to shoot a warning glance at the DI, but he was gratified to see from Harvey's expression that he too had grasped the situation.

Leric used the hall extension, speaking softly into the white telephone as he gave DC Veitch instructions to bring out the CRO portraits.

Within half an hour Irene Spauling had positively identified Crouper and Sand as the two men who had called on her husband.

The sweet smell rising from the wet lawns helped Harvey to relax after the tense atmosphere in the house. He walked back to the car with Leric and got into the passenger seat.

'A turn-up, that, gaffer.' The Sergeant started the engine. 'I never thought Irene'd cough.'

Harvey looked back at the house. 'I don't reckon they ever meant to kill him, just teach him a lesson, like the others, only they went that bit too far. She's a bitter woman and there's no accounting for that.'

Leric turned the car out of the driveway. 'Shall we pull them in, then?'

Harvey smiled. 'We'll do better than that. I had the report on Spauling's clothes before we left. They found traces of iron oxide, so he must have been burnt with the thermic lance.'

Leric's face tightened. 'What about Irene? I don't think she's realized yet what she's let herself in for and I don't suppose she cares any more, but we'll need her in one piece.'

Harvey hadn't overlooked the danger to the woman : 'We'll put a round-the-clock watch on the house, I'll get McKenzie on to it.' He leaned back in his seat as the car headed towards the city. 'And in the meantime, you get a couple of warrants ready. We'll have that Ford Mustang brought in and Spauling's garage turned over, then we'll see what we've got. I want this lot wrapped up nice and tight.'

CHAPTER XII

THE LONDONERS clinched the deal themselves, in cash. Ever since they had arrived in the City, they had been looking for suitable property from which their business could operate without arousing suspicion. The betting shop was an ideal front. The comings and goings of the 'collectors' would pass unnoticed among the punters, and all the 'pensions' transactions could easily be disguised in the accounts. They had picked the shop with care; it was behind a shopping precinct with a big crowded car park, accessible through front and rear entrances, and the flat above meant that it could be guarded day and night. The legitimate purchase of the property would save them from any future embarrassment and the estate agent had accepted the thick wad of notes paid as a deposit, without raising an eyebrow. He was used to dealing with bookmakers and their like, and tax fiddles were none of his concern. It was the way bookies worked, hard cash transactions and no traceable cheques.

Crouper, Brady and Sand had spent much of the day at the betting shop, preparing the new headquarters for the operators who would take over the vice, corruption and protection rackets.

On the way back into town Crouper stopped the car to buy a copy of the local evening newspaper, leafing through the pages as he walked back to the car. Spauling's death was front page news.

'Shit,' said Crouper viciously, 'that bastard Spauling's croaked.'

Sand snatched the paper and read the report closely. 'That's all we needed,' he said, handing the crumpled sheet to Brady. 'Bloody great. If he spilled his guts to the law before he died, we're in dead lumber.'

Brady threw the newspaper on the back seat, unruffled by the fact that he had claimed another life. 'If he'd talked,' he reasoned, 'we'd have had some law at the garage by now. Spauling's not the type, he wouldn't tell the coppers the time while he stood a chance of having a crack for himself. The papers says he was recovering when he copped pneumonia.'

Crouper spat out of the open window. 'They'll turn it over now, though, that's for sure.'

Brady nodded. 'Get on to Harper and find out.'

Crouper left the car again and walked over to a pavement telephone kiosk. He closed the heavy door behind him, lifted the receiver and dialled the number of

Spauling's showroom. Harper would be all right, he thought; although he was one of Spauling's men, he had soon changed sides when he saw the strength, and had even tried to bribe one of the local D's for them with the old 'give your wife a treat' chat, only the copper had been too stupid to stand still for the drop.

Crouper's palms were sweating as he gripped the telephone. Was it going to ring for ever? A voice he didn't recognise answered with just the number, and Crouper was tempted to hang up for every instinct told him that it was the police at the other end of the line.

He fought down the desire. 'Is that Bridge Street Motors?' he asked in a neutral tone.

'Yes,' came the curt reply.

'Can I speak to Mr Harper, please?'

'Mr Harper?'

'Yes, that's right, Mr Allan Harper in the showroom.'

'Who's calling?' asked the flat copper's voice.

'My name's Jackson,' said Crouper, snapping up the first name that came to mind.

'Hang on, will you.'

He had dialled the direct line number deliberately, so that he could not be overheard on the switchboard. The sound of footsteps filled the earpiece and Crouper recognized the man who picked up the telephone as the car salesman.

'Hallo, who's that?'

'Call me Jackson and act natural, I'm a customer, remember?' Crouper said swiftly.

Harper caught on quickly. 'What can I do for you, squire . . . ?'

'You got the law there?'

'Yeah, that's right, about a dozen different models.'

Crouper swore softly, sweating freely now. 'They turning the place over?'

'Oh yeah, you're right there. I've been a bit busy myself.'

There was the sound of someone else talking in the background, and then Harper's voice. 'Hang on a minute, will you, mate?' More muffled conversation, and the sound of a door closing.

Harper came back, speaking softly now. 'He's gone down to the others. You'd better keep away, the place is crawling with coppers.'

'We just heard Spauling croaked,' Crouper said flatly. 'Act like you don't know nothing and we'll see you all right.'

'You said it, squire,' replied the salesman. 'I only work here, don't I?'

'They'll be watching you, son,' Crouper warned. 'Don't do anything you might regret.'

'Do me a favour, I've got the picture.'

'We'll be in touch, then, but next time I'll call you at home. In the meantime, keep your ears and eyes open.' Crouper put the phone down and wiped his hands on his handkerchief. Christ, he thought, I'm sweating like a bull. He opened the door and gulped in fresh air before going back to the car.

The others were silent, waiting. 'You're right.' He turned to Brady in the back seat. 'The law's moved in, but they could stick what they find up their noses and it won't make 'em sneeze. Just a few empty bottles, that's all.'

Sand had been thinking it out. 'What about the

lance?' His voice rose as he turned to Brady. 'You left the
bleedin' lance in there, didn't you, you stupid . . .'

'Forget it,' Brady cut in. 'It's in the workshop with
the welding and cutting gear, and that's just what the
law will think it is, another acetylene torch. They've
never seen a thermic lance up here, so they won't
suss nothing.'

'You sure?' Crouper's eyes narrowed.

'I know,' Brady replied. 'If we'd left it in the van, then
they might have started wondering what it was, but in
the workshop with the welding kit, it don't look nothing
out of the ordinary. It's the best hiding place there
is, coppers or no coppers.'

'All right,' said Crouper, satisfied. 'Now we've got to
move fast before the law starts fouling things up. We'd
better put the arm on Farrow right away so that we can
get off out of it back to town.' He thought for a
moment, gazing through the windscreen. 'Lincoln, the
doorman down the You-Too knows him, they used to be
mates. We'll get him to set Barney up.' He started the
car and they drove back to the betting shop to prepare
for the negotiations with Barney Farrow.

It had not been difficult to recruit Max Lincoln. He'd
been an easy touch, prey for the sadists and perverts of
his own homosexual world. Lincoln had been wide
open to pressure and had needed little persuasion to
ally himself to the Londoners. There had been about a
score of easy ones among the local underworld, prepared
to sell out to whoever was on top; they had been
conscripted as the labourers, turning on their former
fraternity brothers who had resisted the persuaders.

Numerous battles had taken place in the clubs and alleyways of the city; dirty fights which ended with a broken bottle in the face or groin, and the hard core of the opposition had been crushed systematically until all but a handful had either changed sides or had fled from the city to lick their wounds. Of the villains, only Barney Farrow was left who mattered to the London mob. With Jack inside, he was the quartermaster of the Mace firm, the keeper of the archives of extortion and corruption on which the operation was founded. Once Farrow succumbed, their take-over would be complete.

Lincoln sat in his Mini parked outside the block of flats, waiting for Farrow to arrive and passing the time chain-smoking Gauloises and admiring his reflection in the driving mirror. He had chosen his black leather coat for the occasion and frequently flicked a fine stainless steel comb through his blond hair. The comb had become one of his trade marks, for in all his clothes he had provided a narrow pocket for it, right beside an identical slit in the lining in which he carried a slim stiletto. Many a queer-hater had reached, stunned, for his gashed face and felt the hot blood running between his fingers from the effects of the blade.

It was getting dark and shadows were already reaching across the access drive as lights went on in the flats; soon he would be unable to see himself in the little mirror and that would upset him. Lincoln bit his lip. He liked to be surrounded by mirrors, in his flat he even had them on the bathroom ceiling. It comforted him to be able to see his own image multiplied in the silver-backed glass. He lit another cigarette from the stub of the last one. It had been living hell in prison and the thought of going back inside made him shudder. Certainly the male community provided all the attention he could hope for to slake his perverted appetite; the third man in the cell turning his face to the wall while he, Lincoln, slipped into the arms of the second inmate and forgot the sweat and the stench of urine. But he had been denied a mirror and that almost drove him insane. Lincoln had polished his skilly until it gleamed, but the reflection had been distorted and he had earned himself a week in the chokey wing by hurling the offending bucket from the gallery, in a fit of pique. He doubted if he would ever be able to stand another prison sentence, it would turn him into a gibbering wreck.

Lincoln reached inside his coat, letting his fingertips enjoy the rich coolness of the leather before seeking out the knife in a small reflex of reassurance, then he took out his comb again and in the fading light peered at his face in the mirror. In the background he saw a blue Jaguar turn off the road and park outside the flats. He waited until Farrow had crossed to the lighted entrance hall before leaving the Mini and following, treading lightly on the paving stones until he was inside the foyer. He gave Barney time to reach his second-floor flat and then recalled the lift and pressed the indicator button.

Lincoln took his bearings on the landing, remembering his last visit to the place when he had helped lay on some girls for a party; that had gone against the grain but Farrow had paid him well for his services. He walked up to the flat door and noticed a new addition—a Chubb wide-angle peephole had been fitted since his last visit. Cheeky, thought Lincoln, smiling, you're getting artful in your old age, aren't you, lover. He

H

pressed the bell, holding the palm of his other hand over the viewer.

'Who is it?' He recognized Farrow's voice behind the door.

'Max Lincoln. You remember little Maxie, don't you, sweetie?'

'What do you want?'

'Come on, Barney, open up, it's draughty out here—I'll catch my death.'

The door jerked open suddenly and a hand grabbed his lapel, closing the route to the knife pocket. Farrow was an old hand all right.

Lincoln smiled at the angry scowl on the other man's face. 'Hey, steady,' he mocked, as Farrow twisted him off balance against the wall. 'Don't be so aggresive, old love.'

'What do you want, Lincoln?' Farrow growled again, pulling the blond-haired man inside and slamming the door with his foot. 'And don't come any crap with me or I'll break your bloody neck before you can reach the chiv.'

Lincoln leaned against the wall and raised his arms high. 'Just a friendly visit, Barney, no need to get rough, I'm not going to hurt you,' and he winked, 'I've brought you a message, that's all. Some friends of yours from London want to see you—urgent.'

So this was it. Farrow felt a chill like the one which had seized him in the mortuary and his fingers tightened on the soft black leather.

'Leave off,' Lincoln cried, suddenly alarmed, 'you'll ruin my coat.'

'When?' Farrow snapped, feeling the blood pounding through his veins.

'Chucking out time tonight.'

'Where?' He spat the monosyllable.

'The Three Feathers' car park—drive in at half past ten and wait, they'll come to you.'

'The Three Feathers on the Broadway?'

'That's the one, lover. Oh, and they said to come alone, they don't like a crowd.'

Barney opened the door with his free hand and pushed Lincoln out on to the landing. 'OK, Maxie, message delivered. Now you go back and tell them I don't like pansies as messenger boys. If they want to talk business, they know the phone number. I'll be waiting.'

The door slammed and Lincoln straightened out his creased lapel. I'd do time for you Barney, he thought hotly, I'd do a stretch to see you marked, pushing me about. He reached for the knife by instinct, and then the memories of the prison scenes cautioned him and he swallowed hard. It wasn't worth it, not now.

Farrow went back into the living-room of the flat and forced himself to stop turning over the possibilities in his mind. The Londoners would contact him soon enough, the opening gambit of sending Lincoln was proof of that. He loosened his tie and stretched out on the wide chesterfield, a bottle of Vat 69 at his elbow. Farrow watched the purple night darken in the oblong of the window and presently he drew the curtains, switched on a table lamp and poured himself a drink.

He had never been much of a planner, content to leave the scheming to Jack Mace, and without his boss, Barney felt bereft. The old gambits had been all right for a troublesome customer; there weren't many who could stand a good pasting more than once, a nicely balanced brawl in a nightspot, a few bricks from a passing car, or for the more stubborn, a shotgun blast through the letterbox. The old methods hadn't worked with the Londoners, and Farrow had been helpless to resist as his men were picked off one by one. He was out of his depth, but still important enough for the Londoners to tackle him with care. I've still got a few cards to play, Farrow thought ruefully, enough to keep my skin if I'm cunning enough. They'll want the operation intact if they can get it, and I'm the only one who can give it to them on a plate. Make no mistake about it, you bastards, I've still got enough pull in this town to make it tough on you. Without my contacts, you'll start from scratch and that'll cost you plenty, whoever you are.

That was the part which really rankled with him, the fact that despite all the resources he had been able to draw together, he still didn't know a single name. It could be the biggest con of all time, thought Farrow, a couple of wide boys on the make. He dismissed the possibility in the same instant. No, these fingers were dead crafty, treading lightly, moving about and leaving nothing to chance. He would learn their identities when they were good and ready, not before.

The white telephone on the window sill roused him, and Barney picked up the instrument, speaking softly.

'Hallo, Barney,' said a voice he didn't recognize. 'You won't know me, but we've got a mutual friend, old son : Max Lincoln. He does little jobs for us.'

So this was them. Farrow felt his throat go dry as he searched back through his memory, trying to place the voice. It was no good.

'You upset Max tonight, Barney boy, he was only doing what he was told.'

'If you've got something to say,' Farrow began, 'you'd better get on with it.'

The voice laughed, a mirthless sound. 'You count yourself lucky. We don't usually bother with invites, not in our line of business.'

'Forget the sharp chat and get on with it—who the 'ell are you anyway?'

'Never mind the names, cock, they don't matter. There's only one bloke you ought to know about, Alex Shapiro—mean anything?'

Farrow drew a long breath, carefully, so that it would not be heard over the phone. So that was the set-up —Shapiro, hard man of the East End. He might have guessed.

'What if it does?'

'Well, we look after things for Mr Shapiro, make sure he gets what he wants, so to speak.'

'So what's it to me, then?'

'Come off it,' said the voice, 'you're not stupid, Farrow. You know how many beans make five. Mr Shapiro reckons it's time you stepped aside. Nothing personal, but you're in the way, and from where I'm standing, you got no choice, so why don't you do what Lincoln told you and be reasonable.'

'Because,' replied Farrow flatly, 'I like to choose my own deals. I don't take orders from queers, and anyway, a pub car park late at night? You must think I was born yesterday.'

'Look,' said the voice, 'we could knock you off any time we wanted to, only Mr Shapiro reckons you're a reasonable man, the sort who might talk business.'

'I've only got your word for that.'

'Name your own place, if you're that worried. We just want a friendly chat.'

Farrow thought quickly. 'All right,' he said, 'the Empire Sporting Club, in the bar at seven tomorrow night.'

'Suits me. You'll be alone of course?'

'Yes—so will you.'

'What makes you so sure?' It was the caller's turn to ask the questions.

'It's members only. I'll leave you an invite at the door in the name of Mister . . . ?' he let the question trail.

'Jackson,' said the voice, 'Mister Jackson.'

The receiver clicked on the other end of the line and Farrow replaced the telephone, a tight smile on his lips. He'd have them on his own terms, by Christ.

Farrow made sure he arrived at the club in plenty of time. He was well known there, respected as a member of some standing. The doorman parked his Jaguar in the private car park and Farrow went on into the club and sought out Saunders, the manager.

'I'm expecting a guest tonight, Tom,' he said, hanging up his light overcoat in the members' cloakroom, 'a Mr Jackson. He'll be arriving about seven o'clock; I'll be in the bar if you'll show him up.'

Saunders smiled, a carefully groomed movement of his mouth. You had to look after the members, especially one like Mr Farrow who had helped keep the club alive by sponsoring one or two bouts every now and again.

'Leave it to me, I'll make sure he finds you.'

Farrow made his way up the wide staircase, glancing at the now familiar row of photographs depicting famous wrestlers in action. The bar was a copy of a Victorian gentlemen's club, except that the comfortable hide chairs were really simulated leather and the oak-panelled walls just wood veneer. Instead of *Country Life* and the *Financial Times*, the newspaper rack held copies of *The Ring* and *Sporting Life*. He settled for a large gin and tonic and found himself a chair facing the door beside a small card table. Cigar smoke drifted in the air from a poker school in one corner of the room and a couple of dedicated drinkers were chatting idly at the bar.

He clipped the tip of a Panatella, rolled the cigar between his lips and lit it, waiting for the tobacco to glow before replacing it in his mouth. He blew a thin stream of smoke and dropped the match into a squat brass ashtray. It was necessary that his image should be just right; that the Londoner he was to meet should know from the start that he was not dealing with one of the strong-arm mugs, but with an influential member of the fraternity.

Farrow glanced at his watch. It was five minutes past seven. Come on, you bastard, he swore softly to himself, feeling the tension beginning to tighten in his neck muscles. But he must not get impatient—give the slightest sign of weakness—or he would be finished. He drew deeply on the cigar, feeling the smoke scour his lungs. That's better Barney, take it easy.

Saunders appeared in the doorway and glanced round the room, and Farrow raised his glass in a gesture of recognition, then tipped back the stiff drink to ease the slight uneasiness in his stomach. Barney watched the man walking towards him with the club manager and appraised him carefully. His position had been chosen with care, they would have to cross the room to reach him, giving him time to learn something about the man who called himself Jackson. A dark suit, well cut, stylish; close-cropped hair brushed flat with a little oil; a hard face, shrewd eyes. Good muscles under the jacket; heavy on the neck and waist, a man who'd stop a few punches all right and probably had in his line. A tough joker, thought Farrow, but how tough? He'd know soon enough.

'Mr Jackson for you, Mr Farrow.' The manager bowed slightly as he made the introduction.

Farrow didn't rise and the man smiled down at him, waiting, feet spread slightly, hands hanging loosely at his sides. Could I take him? Farrow left the question unanswered and waved his cigar at a second chair. 'Take the weight off your feet.'

Crouper moved round the card table and slipped into the seat, his eyes never leaving Farrow's face. So this was Barney Farrow, eh? A show of class, a bit of flannel to make him wonder. Well, it didn't cut no ice with him.

'What'll it be?'

'I'll have a scotch with you, Barney.' Crouper glanced around the room. 'Nice little pitch you got yourself here.'

'It does,' Farrow replied non-committally, and he clicked his fingers to catch the barman's attention, calling for the drinks. He turned to find Crouper watching him and recognized the same wariness which would be showing in his own eyes.

The barman set the glasses on the table and Farrow picked up his fresh drink.

'You're a very lucky man, Barney,' Crouper began,

leaning back in his chair. 'When Alex Shapiro wants something, he usually takes it, no asking.'

Farrow watched the man over the rim of the glass. 'Come to buy me off, then, have you?' he asked bluntly.

Crouper sipped his drink. 'Something like that. You see, Mr Shapiro likes your operation—it's got possibilities and he don't care how he gets it.'

'Like knocking off Ted Spauling, you mean.'

Crouper grinned. 'Sorry, I'm just the middle man. I only know that Mr Spauling wasn't very co-operative and he had a bit of an accident, that's all.'

Farrow put the glass down. 'And if I don't co-operate?'

'That would be too bad.' Crouper was still grinning, his eyes bright. 'Do yourself a good turn—get out while you can.'

'What's the drop?'

'We reckoned on ten thou, and no income tax to pay.'

Farrow shook his head, turning down the corners of his mouth. 'Peanuts,' he growled, the gravel quality in his voice grinding the word. 'Without my help, you'll have a hard time setting up in this town. I can still muster enough support to give you a rough ride, and without my clients and the goodwill, so to speak, you'll be starting from scratch.'

'Name a figure, then,' said Crouper.

'Make it fifty and we'll start talking, and remember, that buys you the pensions rounds, the blackmail dope and the extortion squeeze, the whole rake-off.'

Crouper scratched his head. 'You're still talking like a big man, Barney.' He glanced around the bar. 'This don't fool nobody, you know, your organization's finished, you're a has-been.'

Farrow drew on his cigar, forcing himself to smile. 'Don't kid yourself. I haven't even started yet, all you've done is put the wind up the scrubbers. We either deal on my terms or it's a battle. I'm not the bloke who stands in the way of progress, but you'll have to make it worth my while.'

Crouper was thinking quickly. Farrow's attitude was a bit too cocky for his liking. A bluff? Oh sure, it could be, but there was no telling he hadn't done a deal with the law. Crouper remembered another of Shapiro's negotiators, the German, Anton, and the memory made his spine tingle. He had been working on a similar take-over bid in a northern city and the pay-off was being settled over dinner at a hotel, when a waiter came up and offered a silver serving-dish to Anton. He lifted the lid and found a warrant for his arrest under-neath—for demanding money with menaces. The local villains had turned informers to protect their own in-terests, and had set him up for the coppers. The German never stood trial. A team of smart lawyers got him bail and the London mob dealt out their own punishment for failure. Anton had been sentenced to death at a fraternity court martial, and the thermic lance had burnt his body to a cinder, leaving only the charred remains for the fishes in the murky stretches of the River Thames.

'All right, we'll double it. Twenty grand for the whole operation.'

'Not a chance,' replied Farrow flatly. 'I've got the black on some big names in this city, pictures their wives wouldn't like to see, enough to ruin some important careers. It's worth more than that. Tell your boss fifty, and we talk business.'

'I'll have to see what you're offering first.'

'You will—when the price is right.'

Crouper finished his drink. 'All right then, I'll call you tomorrow night.'

Farrow stood, pushed his chair back and looked down at the man. 'You could push your luck too far, Mr Jackson, and get your own fingers burnt.'

Crouper rose, watching Farrow carefully. Keep him sweet, the smooth bastard, he thought. He won't risk losing fifty grand by letting the law in, so I'll just string him along and see what happens.

'Don't worry about us. We've got our own protection. I'll let you know tomorrow.'

Crouper turned and walked across the room without looking back and disappeared through the door.

Farrow watched the empty doorway for several seconds, the dead cigar butt between his fingers.

Farrow found Miller in the second back-street pub he called at, propping up the bar with a half full glass at his elbow and chatting to the shirt-sleeved barman.

He drew him aside and they sat in a narrow booth, their conversation drowned by the din from the juke-box and the clamour of voices in the packed saloon. The air was heavy with the pungent odour of beer, cigarette smoke and human sweat.

'I thought you said we wasn't supposed to be seen together after that last lot,' said Miller quickly, his eyes flicking nervously around the room. 'I've been keeping out of the way ever since Ted copped it, so what's up, Barney?'

Farrow leaned forward, clearing a space among the empty glasses which crowded the small table in a pool of spilt ale, 'I've got a job for you, Miller, and it can't wait. I need a list of all the clients on the squeeze and the blackmail stuff too . . .'

'You want them written down?' Miller asked, staring incredulously at Farrow. 'We never had anything written yet, Barney, Jack would never have stood for it. If the law . . .'

'I know all about that,' Farrow cut in sharply, 'but things have changed.'

'Jack always said we was never to put anything in writing and—'

Anger flared on Farrow's face. 'So what's Jack Mace matter now. He's so bloody smart, he's in the nick for his trouble. I'm telling you Miller, I want it written, got it?'

It cut right across the code, Miller knew that. Mace had never allowed them even to jot down the collections to be made on a particular night, even if the notes were destroyed immediately afterwards. They had to keep the tallies of pensions collected in their heads. Mace had the figures at his fingertips and it was a clout across the face for anyone who was ever a few quid short. He had drummed it into them. The written word, a few figures and names, was as good as a statement to the police and that was unheard of.

'Look, Barney, I don't know about that, it's dead dicey . . .'

But the fury on Farrow's face stilled Miller's tongue. 'You forget Mace. I'm giving the orders now. Jack Mace was so stupid and so greedy that he got himself lumbered with a load of hot gear on him. He wasn't so smart, that's why he's inside. I've had a craw full of Jack Mace.'

Miller said nothing. He had learned only that evening that Mace had been transferred to the city prison for the appeal hearing of his case, and he wondered how his old boss would react if he was sitting in his place. Push a glass in Farrow's face, most likely, to slap him back into line, but then Barney was right, Mace had been a mug, there was no getting away from it, he had been careless enough to get himself knocked off, so maybe his code wasn't perfect after all.

'What do you want me to do then, Barney?'

Farrow had calmed himself after the outburst. 'Just get me the names, one list, no copies, and all the black you're holding.'

'I'll need a couple of days.'

'Make it as quick as you can, and I'll see you all right. It's time we had a bit of a shakedown, things are getting too lax, and this is just the start.'

Farrow knew about the Mace rule, and he had hoped to get Miller's co-operation without arousing too much curiosity; he might have known it wouldn't work. The miserable little bastard didn't have the nous to think for himself, but there was another of Mace's edicts which was working for him. He had been appointed heir to the organization, the undisputed successor should Mace be out of circulation and Miller had no alternative but to follow his orders; Mace had told him to.

CHAPTER XIII

THE BULKY ENVELOPE was burning a hole in his pocket. Miller walked quickly across the landscaped forecourt of the flats and into the entrance hall, his nerves ragged and jumpy. If the law scarf me with this lot, that's me finished, he thought to himself. He had worked fast, writing down a list of the names and places where the weekly collections were made, marking the ones who coughed up easily and the ones who needed leaning on; the clubs, the cafés, billiard halls, the restaurants and back-street betting shops. He had collected the black plastic pouch of photographs and letters from the station locker, using the key Jack Mace had given him, and had stuffed it into the envelope with the list. It had taken twenty-four hours to get everything together and now he just wanted to be rid of it.

Miller got into the lift and went up to Farrow's second-floor flat. If Barney wanted to take the risk, that was up to him, he was the boss now. Miller pressed the bell and waited for Farrow to identify him through the viewer. Come on, hurry it up . . . he pressed the bell again, holding it with his thumb.

Farrow opened the door, standing in the opening, his tie loose at the neck and his face flushed from drink. He had a glass in his hand.

'Come on in—you've got the stuff?'

Miller stepped into the safety of the flat, thankful that the danger was over. 'Right here, Barney.' He took the envelope from his pocket and handed it over.

Farrow walked into the living-room and dropped on to the chesterfield, spilling the contents of the envelope on to a cushion. He read down the list and looked over the rest of the contents, smiling with satisfaction.

'You've done a good job, Miller.' He looked up from the documents. 'What's up? You look like you need a drink, old son.'

'I'm all right, Barney, I didn't fancy carrying it, that's all.' He knew better than to query Farrow's instructions or to ask any more questions after the last angry scene, so he decided to keep his anxiety to himself. If Barney got nicked, then he didn't want any part of it.

'Have a drink and forget it,' said Farrow expansively, sloshing whisky into a second glass. 'This is the start of a new look for this outfit, the mugs are going to wish they'd never been born by the time I've finished with them.'

Farrow dropped the bottle on to the carpet and shook his head to clear the fug of alcohol. He had been drinking steadily all day to bolster his resolve; he had needed to, to save himself from cracking up. There was still time for them to knock him off, if Shapiro gave the word. There would be no phone call, just a knock at the door and a lot of pain before he died. He had to keep them wondering, but right now, he had another job to take care of. It was important that Miller's suspicions were not aroused further, or the whole deal could blow up in his face. Funny—Farrow groped in his memory—he couldn't remember the bloke's first name, he had always been just Miller.

Farrow looked across at him, sitting hunched in his mac, ill at ease on the edge of the armchair. 'Relax, son,' he began, 'it's going to be the gravy train from now on. You just trust old Barney. He laughed suddenly. 'I'm your mate, Miller, remember? This is going to put us on easy street.'

Miller settled himself more comfortably in the chair, but the unease still persisted in his mind. I don't swallow your smooth chat, Barney Farrow, he told himself, from now on, I'm looking after myself. He drained his glass. Whatever Farrow was up to, he was wise enough not to cross him at the moment.

'You're the boss, Barney. I take it we carry on with the collections as usual.'

'Yes, just the same, until you get the word.'

Not likely, thought Miller, once I'm out of here, I'm away. Whatever it is you're scheming, Farrow, I don't want to know.

'We'll show 'em, eh Barney, show 'em they can't push the Mace firm about.'

'That's right.' Farrow grinned. 'Nobody's giving us the bums' rush on our own patch.' Sucker, he thought savagely, you'll wise up after I've been paid off.

The telephone rang, and Farrow drew heavily on the alcohol in his system to keep his face relaxed. He let the phone ring a few times, then rose to answer it, conscious that Miller was watching him. 'It'll be the bird,' he explained with a wink. 'Slip in the kitchen, there's a good lad, and get me another bottle from the cupboard under the sink. The Vat 69.'

Miller didn't seem suspicious and Farrow waited until he was out of the room before lifting the receiver.

'You took your time.'

'I've got company, so make it short. Am I on at the asking price?' Farrow glanced quickly at the kitchen door. He regretted that the call had come while Miller

was in the flat, but he didn't want to delay things
by asking the Londoner to phone again later. He
needed to know at once if the deal was going to work;
he needed time to plan, to make his arrangements to be
far away from this city once he had the money. He
needed a safe bolt-hole in which to lie low in case things
went wrong and they came looking for him. The money
greed gripped him now, but he was smart enough to
make sure he would have the chance to spend it.
Miller was the least of his problems.

'You're on, mate,' said the voice, 'but we'll want
value for money. Sorted out your corner yet?'

In the kitchen, Miller bit his lip as he stood on the
fitted rush matting, glancing quickly around the room;
he knew exactly what he was looking for. A white
flex led to the extension phone in the corner of the
dining alcove. Miller smiled. Now we'll see, Barney, we'll
see who's the mug. He lifted the receiver carefully, hand
over the mouthpiece and recognized Farrow's voice.
You take your risks, Barney, thought Miller, and I'll
take mine. He waited for the caller to speak again.

'The drop'll be in cash and we'll collect at the same
time. We'll want to have a look at your stuff, just to
be on the safe side.'

Miller clenched his teeth. So it wasn't a bird after
all, he hadn't been taken in by that one. That voice
. . . his brow furrowed in concentration. I'd swear I know
that voice from somewhere. Suddenly he felt an in-
explicable twinge of fear.

'That's fair enough. You'll get what you want and no
messing,' Farrow was saying easily. 'You just bring the
money and I'll make sure of the rest.'

'Sooner the better. How about tomorrow?'

I

Miller gripped the telephone tightly. The voice had taken him back, to a darkened scrapyard and he could still smell the burning flesh in his nostrils, feel the iron grip on his arms. It was one of the bastards who'd burned Eddie.

'No,' said Farrow shortly, 'that's too early. There's a few things to be smoothed out, I'll need a bit more time. Make it the day after.'

'We've got all the time in the world,' said the voice, 'only don't make it too long, or Mr Shapiro's likely to get impatient and that means trouble for you, mate.'

'You want it sewn up, don't you? There's a few details outstanding, that's all, they'll have to be squared in both our interests.'

The voice sounded suspicious. 'Don't try any deep games with us, Farrow. I'd as soon put the bite on you, like the others. One more won't make much difference.'

A laugh, slightly nervous. 'You think I'd miss the chance of fifty grand in folding money? I just don't want any after-sales complaints, that's all.'

There was a silence. 'Very commendable,' said the voice finally. 'What do you suggest, then?'

'Give me forty-eight hours and I'll have it all ready. One straight exchange and we're both happy.'

'You'll come to us?'

'Not on your sweet life. I'm not taking the risk of walking about with this stuff on me. You come to me, right here in my place. This is a straight business deal and I don't want any complications.'

'Bit suss, aren't you?' asked the voice mildly.

'Wouldn't you be—after what's been happening?'

A low laugh. 'All right, friend, I'll give you that.

We'll come to you, half past midnight day after to-morrow, and you be alone, Barney, because we'll have help handy, and we'll finish it one way or the other.'

Miller didn't wait for Farrow's reply. He set the phone back on the rest and took a deep breath to calm himself, then he moved to the wall cabinet, opening all the cupboard doors in sight. The phone pinged and he knew the conversation was over. Miller opened the door below the sink and reached inside; his hand closed around the distinctive whisky bottle and he stood up to see Farrow leaning on the door jamb.

'Come on, Miller, I'm getting a thirst.'

He handed over the bottle and watched as Farrow stripped off the seal, then turned and closed the cup-boards. 'I was looking for the soda, Barney . . .'

'It's in here.' Farrow turned into the living-room and Miller took another deep breath. He still thinks I'm a mug . . . well, he'll learn. He followed Barney and found him pouring two fresh drinks.

'Get this down you, son. To the new firm.'

Miller swallowed the hot liquor and felt the jolt in his stomach.

Farrow had crossed the room and was opening a drawer in the oak bureau. 'You've done a good job, Miller,' he was saying, his back turned to the other man. 'Here's a little bonus,' Farrow began peeling fivers from a thick wad. 'A ton to be going on with, and there's plenty more where that came from. When we're in business again, there'll be no stopping us.' He pushed the money into Miller's hand, £100 in crisp notes.

Miller feigned pleasure. 'You've always done right by me, boss, I've got no complaints.'

Farrow topped up the glasses again and they drank

in silence. So what if Miller had guessed, thought Farrow, money's the only language he knows, and I've bought him. He won't go to the law, not with his form, and there isn't anybody else. Besides, in two days' time, I'll be long gone. He laughed expansively. 'Sup up then, there's plenty of booze too.' Farrow was watching him narrowly; if Miller was suspicious, the drink would find him out.

He poured another liberal measure into the two tumblers, the bottle now half empty.

Miller struggled to keep the turmoil inside him out of sight, and found the alcohol was working for him rather than against. He let the words slur slightly, pretending that the drink had loosened his tongue.

'Nice little drum you've got here, Barney. Nothing but the best, eh? I reckon I'll fix myself up with a place like this, I'm sick of living out of a suitcase. I'll bet it works wonders with the skirts.'

That's right, thought Farrow, you get yourself well oiled, my little friend, and then we'll see what's what.

'It does,' he replied, anxious to preserve Miller's mellow mood, 'you show the birds a good time and you've got it made.' He leered suggestively. Come on, you little git, drink up.

'Costs a packet, though,' said Miller, deliberately letting his eyelids droop; inside his mind was crystal clear.

'Like I said, there's plenty of bunse for both of us, you'll do all right.'

They had been drinking quickly, swopping measure for measure of the high proof spirit, each clinging to sobriety and fannying the other. Miller could see the high flush creeping over Farrow's face and he felt the time would soon come when Barney would bring up the subject of the phone call.

'Take that little darling,' said Farrow, waving his glass at the telephone, 'She can't get enough of it. Wanted to see me tonight, only I said I was too busy.' He watched Miller artfully, ready to pounce at the slightest reaction, but there was none, not even a tiny tightening of the stupid, slack, grinning mouth.

'You should have told her to bring a friend,' Miller slurred admiringly.

The moment was over. Farrow erased any threat from Miller with a broad grin. Too stupid to come in out of the rain. I might have known. This caper's got me jumping at shadows.

Miller put his glass down on the table and rose unsteadily. 'I'll be off now, then, Barney. I've got a dolly of me own to sort out. Not high-class like your birds —but you've got to grab what you can.'

Farrow saw him to the door. 'Forget her,' he advised as Miller moved toward the door, 'throw a little money about and get yourself something a bit special for tonight, you've earned it. Here—' he took a slip of paper out of his wallet and gave it to Miller—'forget the brasses, that's a real high-class call girl. Have yourself a good time and I'll look you up at the week-end, then we can really start operating again.'

Miller got into the lift and pressed the ground-floor button. The door hummed shut and he gave way to the uncontrollable shaking, leaning heavily against the lift wall. You double-dyed bastard, Farrow, he whispered and repeated the phrase over and over like a prayer.

Joseph Silverbach stuck a slip of paper in the heavy

volume of criminal law reports to mark the page and closed the book. He made a pencil mark in the margin of the closely typed transcript page which was open on his study desk and pushed that aside too; the green card cover bearing the heading Reg. v Mace flipped shut. It was already nine o'clock, and the little Jewish lawyer had spent the past two hours checking over the arguable aspects of Mace's appeal for the barrister he had briefed to put before the Assize judge. With a bit of luck they might make some ground on misdirection of the jury, but somehow Silverbach doubted it. Mace had already got off lightly and all the legal double talk in the fat tomes he had taken from the Law Library couldn't evade the plain facts on which the jury had reached their verdict.

He took off his black-rimmed reading glasses, the ones he always wore in court with the morning jacket and pin-striped trousers, and rolled his shirt-sleeves down, fitting the gold chain-links back in the cuffs. He leaned back in the scuffed brown leather chair and yawned, reflecting that Jack Mace was indeed an important client, for there were few cases nowadays which intruded on Silverbach's leisure time. He had a couple of junior partners to handle the bulk of the case load. Silverbach had inherited the family law firm and had promptly set about taking the hard work out of his career by transforming the staid old-established firm of solicitors into a sort of legal supermarket, specializing in criminal work and milking the legal aid system for all it was worth. He had the simple philosophy that a cheap villain who couldn't afford to defend himself was hardly likely to kick up a fuss when the State was paying for whatever sort of defence he received. As long as he convinced them he was on their side, with a few impassioned pleas before the bench, he was on to a soft number, and even a strongly worded complaint to the Law Society from a rather more dedicated member of the profession protesting that Silverbach was just a manipulator of the law, had done nothing more than increase his stature with the criminal fraternity.

Jack Mace had been altogether different. He had wanted a lawyer on call twenty-four hours a day to protect his interests, and the retainer he had offered had been far too tempting for Silverbach to refuse. Over the years they had become something akin to partners, and on more than one occasion, Silverbach had risked professional disgrace while working for Mace. It was a partnership founded on hard cash.

His wife broke into his reflections, standing in the doorway of his study, a small dark plump woman who knew nothing of his business except that it enabled them to live the sort of life that was expected of a professional man of the Hebrew faith.

'What is it, my dear?' He rose from his chair and reached for his jacket.

'There is someone at the door to see you, Joseph—a Mr Miller.'

Silverbach had a good memory for names and he knew of Miller as a *chaver* of Jack Mace, a man he had met often in their dealings. He shrugged.

'It is late for him to call.' His wife looked worried.

'Business, my dear.' The lawyer patted her shoulder. 'Bring him up, I will not be so long.'

All the same, he thought, as his wife retraced her steps, it was a strange hour for such a visit. He tidied up the papers he had been working on, slipped them into the desk drawer and locked it. It was unwise to take any chances. His wife showed Miller into the study and closed the door discreetly.

'Ah, Mr Miller.' Silverbach crossed the room and shook hands with his visitor. 'There is something I can do for you that is so urgent you must come to my home?'

But for the monthly cheque, thought Silverbach, I would never tolerate such inconsideration, but then, Mace was a generous man and so . . .

'Sit down, Mr Miller, and tell me what is on your mind.'

Miller glanced nervously around the wall bookshelves. 'I've got to get in touch with Jack. You were the only person I could think of, Mr Silverbach . . . the only one who can reach him in the nick.'

Silverbach looked puzzled. 'I have access to my client, naturally, but I don't see . . .'

'Look, Mr Silverbach—' he could see that Miller's hands were shaking—'I got to get a message to Jack, it's very important.'

Silverbach scratched his head. Something was wrong, and he had no desire to get himself involved. 'It would be most irregular. I am an officer of the court.'

'Yes, I know all about that chat,' Miller cut in quickly, 'but you've bent the rules before and I wouldn't ask if it wasn't important—it's something Jack's got to know.' He looked agitated. 'Jack'll see you're all right, it's that urgent.'

Silverbach considered the request carefully. He could not afford to upset Mace, he was a lucrative client. 'What is it you wish me to do, my friend?'

'When will you see Jack again?'

'Tomorrow morning. I have an appointment to take instructions for his appeal. I shall be visiting him in the prison.'

'There's something I want you to tell him. You can do that, can't you, being his lawyer, like?'

Silverbach pursed his lips and leaned back in his chair. 'Say no more, my friend. As his legal adviser, I am in a delicate position. I must have no knowledge of any— well, let us say, irregularities, for want of a better word. If I were discovered in the role of a courier, then—' he raised a hand in a delicate gesture—'I would no longer be of use to Mr Mace. I must think of my position. All I can suggest—' Silverbach opened a drawer low down in the desk and took out a sheet of statement paper—'is that you write a message for Mr Mace on one of these additional evidence papers, and I will show it to him with the rest of the statements we have prepared for the hearing.' Silverbach pushed the sheet of paper across the desk and frowned. 'But I must warn you, my friend. I cannot know what you have written.'

Miller nodded. 'As long as Jack sees it, that's all that matters. I knew I could count on you, Mr Silverbach, you're a real gent.'

Silverbach watched Miller hunched over the edge of the desk, writing laboriously between the ruled lines, totally engrossed in the wording of the message. Today, he thought ruefully, I still have a few vestiges of respect. Tomorrow? He pushed the whimsical speculation from his mind; what good were fine ideals of law without money? He had chosen his own road to justice.

Miller filled half the page with close spiky writing and

laid down the pen as if a weight had been taken from his shoulders. He smiled for the first time. 'Give that to Jack, Mr Silverbach, and tell him I'm waitin'. You won't regret it, take it from me.'

CHAPTER XIV

THE DAWN SKY was a candy stripe of high cirrus, striated by the first sepia rays of the sun. They awakened the long angular shadows which were the constant companions of tall city buildings. Here and there, a blind window high on the glass façade of an office block winked back at the new day.

The quiet streets were already coming to life with bright-coloured delivery vans disgorging bundles of morning newspapers at the pavement stands. A mechanical road-sweeper left a wet trail in the gutters, its brushes rotating noisily in the quietness.

Leric scrubbed at the bristle on his chin with the back of his hand, and regretted he had not had time to shave. He drove quickly across the city centre and on into the side-streets, the car wheels shuddering on the uneven concrete blocks of the road surface. He turned into Bridge Street and drove up to the front of the motor showroom, parking the car at the kerbside. A greasy chip paper fluttered in the gutter as a gentle breeze began to pick up the first scraps of flotsam which littered the streets.

Leric took a bunch of keys from his mac pocket and unlocked the new shiny police padlock on the showroom door. Spauling's place had been sealed off after the first search, locked and barred by the uniformed men who had followed the local detectives. Leric had chosen the morning because he wanted the place to himself; when he had time to think before the clear crystals of his mind became clouded by the many chemical reactions of the job which would begin the minute he walked into the squad office and signed his name in the duty book. Only at this ungodly hour, without the clumsy efforts of his superiors to distract his attention, did he have the chance to give his own ideas full rein.

The detective glanced around the bare offices, the chairs pushed carefully against the walls, and everything from the window-sills to the door knobs, coated with the white dust of the fingerprint men. There would be nothing for him there. He went to the rear of the building, down a short flight of steps to the workshops and stopped, hands on hips, taking in the whitewashed walls and the tools scattered on the work benches. Above his head, a chain pulley hung down from a beam and the floor underneath was badly oil-stained. Come on, come on, Leric urged himself impatiently, think about it. It's got to be here, it's the only logical place. It fits the pattern, and because it fits, it's got to be right.

He began again, starting from the doorway where he had entered, standing perfectly still and using his eyes to probe the recesses in the room. He would look more closely presently, but first he wanted to get the feel of the place, study the lay-our and give his experience of the job a chance to lead him to what he was certain he would find somewhere in the garage—something the local lads could have tripped over without realizing the significance. The fingerprints had been a start, two on a carelessly disposed whisky bottle and a half thumb on a desk drawer; they were being checked with the CRO. Sitxteen comparisons on the whorls and loops would be needed before they could be used in evidence. What Leric had in mind was something far more conclusive. 'And it's right here in this bloody garage, I'll stake my rep on it,' he murmured aloud.

There was only one sure way to outwit Chummy, he had learned, and that was to think like him, know with absolute certainty which way he would jump . . . You had to be able to walk down a street you'd never seen before and pick out Chummy's house just by the hang of the curtains; you had to know his habits, his boozer, his corner café, his birds. You had to be Chummy, for as long as it took to catch him out. The Londoners would be the same, they would think the same and react in the same way. Chummy seldom changed.

Leric played it out again in his mind, step by step through the pattern which had preoccupied him ever since the warehouse fire. *I would dump it in the cut, the best place, nobody would ever find it under ten feet of filthy canal ooze. Play it safe and dump it. Why? Think about it. Nobody's sussed a thing yet, more than likely they won't catch on either. I'll hang on to it for the time being, no sense in jumping the gun, plenty of time to get rid of it if things start getting hot. Nothing, I told you so, the coppers up here haven't connected. Probably missed it altogether, there's nothing to worry about, safe as houses. Wait. Better be on the safe side, just in case. Give me a bit of breathing space. Hide it, somewhere inconspicuous.*

Where? Leric stared at a dark recess hidden by shadows at the far end of the workshop. Where it wouldn't be noticed, of course. Where it would just look like the rest of the gear, perfectly innocuous.

He walked quickly across the floor, pulling on a pair of leather gloves in case there were further prints to be had there. Chummy would have walked this floor before him, planning and scheming. The workbench had been treated to only a cursory examination, Leric could see that, for the tools were where they would have been left, but invoices and papers on an old metal working surface which served as a desk had been pushed aside and the drawers and telephone extension on top dusted for latents.

In the wide bay he found two gas cylinders standing side by side, one much taller than the other, a tangle of rubber hose connecting them to cutting torches held in a wall clip. Behind them, Leric found a small trolley on wide rubber wheels which carried the portable welding kit, two smaller gas cylinders in a metal tray between the tubular uprights of the cradle. The detective stooped to examine the tray. It had corroded with a light film of rust, but where the left-hand cylinder stood a bright ring of metal was exposed, for the imprint was slightly larger than the base of the cylinder. Now that was very interesting. Leric unhooked the hose from the trolley cleats and uncovered a black-painted adaptor with a hand wheel-valve in the middle and a threaded nozzle. He hefted the adaptor in one hand and studied the cylinders for a long minute before he saw the deception. Both cylinders were of identical size and shape, but the maroon paint identifying the acetylene bottle was unscratched. Leric took a penknife from his pocket and scraped a flake of paint from the curve of the container. Underneath, the paint was black. They both contained oxygen, but someone had taken care to disguise the fact with a coat of new paint.

Leric smiled as he locked the last piece into the jigsaw. It was worthy of me laddo, he thought; who would ever suspect a welding kit as being anything other than it appeared? Not Landon's lads, certainly, not many of the D's who worked by the book. You had to get inside Chummy's mind to catch him out.

He cut his hand emptying the scrap metal bin which was piled high with the debris of car body repairs, but from a tangle of swarf, he recovered a length of gas barrel packed with the rods he had seen in the stub at the Forensic Lab. He placed it carefully on the work-bench and went back into the office, well satisfied. He glanced at his watch, it was still very early, then picked up the telephone and dialled Colin Harvey's home number and listened to the phone ringing. The DI answered, his voice heavy from sleep.

'Mornin', gaffer.' Leric didn't try to hide the elation in his voice. 'Bit of good news.' He grinned at Harvey's puzzled reply. 'Thought I'd have another look at Spauling's place in case Landon's boys missed anything.' He paused and waited for Harvey to ask. 'I've found the thermic lance.'

CHAPTER XV

THE PRISON was very old, very cramped and very primitive. The city had expanded around it, and now the crumbling greystone perimeter wall which hid the rusty corrugated roofs of the workshops and the barred slit

windows of the cell blocks was less than three miles
from the big brash department stores and the commercial
heart of the city.

Joseph Silverbach parked his car in a side-street opposite the main gate and waited for the traffic to clear
before crossing the main road, briefcase tucked under his
arm.

An untidy queue of prison officers, key chains dangling
below their tunic jackets, filed one by one through the narrow wicket gate set in the big door. Silverbach joined the
shuffling line, glancing at the rusty studs in the door and
the worn grimy façade of the castellated gatehouse which
were the only breaks in the wall. Even in the height of
summer, it was always cold and dank inside the prison,
and Silverbach, who had made many such visits in his
professional capacity, knew with an awful certainty that
he would be insane within a week in such confinement.

He answered the warder's final questions and stood
by the small gate as his name was checked on the
official list.

'All right, sir.' He motioned the lawyer inside. 'The
Chief Officer will be down directly to take you through.'

'Thank you—you are very kind.' Silverbach bobbed
his head and stood on the uneven flagstones looking
through the gatehouse grille into the central courtyard.
He knew the Chief Officer slightly, a tall man with
iron-grey hair and a not unkind face, and when he
arrived, buttoning the jacket of his uniform, the lawyer
was relieved. He would be glad to be back in the
sunshine.

He was taken to the interview room beyond the
prison offices where a warder was waiting beside the
door. Silverbach thanked them and went inside. Jack

Mace was sitting behind the table in the centre of the room in which two hard-backed chairs completed the furnishings.

'Good morning, Mr Mace.'

'Hallo, Joe.' Mace nodded at the other chair. 'Take a pew.'

Silverbach laid his briefcase on the table. 'It would be more fitting,' he began mildly, 'if you were to use my surname, in the circumstances.' He glanced at the closed door.

Mace laughed. 'The screws, you mean? Don't worry about them, mate, they won't give us no bother.'

Silverbach shrugged and sat down.

'Well now,' said Mace leaning forward, 'what you got to tell me? Am I going to do me bird, or kiss goodbye to this hole?'

Silverbach opened his case and took out the file of documents. 'Your appeal will be heard the day after tomorrow, but I'm bound to tell you that our case is pretty slim.'

'Never mind, me old darlin', you'll do your best, eh? No sense in havin' a good client like me rotting away in the nick.' That was about the size of it, Mace reflected bitterly, do your bird nice and steady, wait for your remission; the brown paper bag with your gear stuffed inside, and the eight o'clock walk through the big gates to freedom. Four bleedin' years. Never again. The next time it'll be a lagging, and a pension book when I come out. You had to have a knock, but he didn't expect too much from the appeal judge. They had been waiting for Jack Mace too long. The quiet smiles on the coppers' faces instead of the table-bashing interrogation sessions; the line-up for the police photographer in the central lock-up after the first remand when he'd sucked his cheeks in and stared wide-eyed at the camera to make his mug smudge as unrealistic as possible. He'd known from then that there'd be no wriggling out of this one, scarfed bang to rights, and all because he fell for the smooth chat of a bunch of operators who wouldn't see a tickle if it was under their noses.

Silverbach was shuffling through a sheaf of papers taken from his briefcase.

'I reckon you're right at that,' Mace said soberly. 'They've got me tied up with ribbon on this one, haven't they?'

Silverbach nodded, his face grave. 'A lawyer can do so much, Jack, but with the evidence . . .' He shrugged his shoulders in a gesture of hopelessness.

Mace bit his thumbnail. 'Yeah, I know. Still, I've had a fairy to meself in the remand wing on the strength; next week the tea-party's over, though, it'll be back to three in a cell on the moor for yours truly.'

Silverbach pushed a paper across the table. 'I had a caller last night. A friend of yours who wanted to get a message to you urgently. He was very excited and I told him he had better write it as a statement. That is what he wrote.'

Silverbach felt a curious hypnotism grip him as he watched Mace read the statement and saw the light blue eyes scanning Miller's scrawl slowly harden to the grey of granite, as if a chemical reaction were taking place behind them. The man's face closed like a clenched fist, two deep fissures running down to the corners of his

K

mouth and draining the blood from his lips. Lips which drew back in a tight dangerous smile. Mace pushed the statement back across the table.

'Got a fag?' he said suddenly.

Silverbach fumbled in his jacket pocket, found the cigarettes, and gave one to Mace and lit it for him. Although he rarely smoked, Silverbach took one himself to ease the tightening of his nerves. Whatever Mace had learned from Miller's message, it spelled trouble, and he was right in the firing line.

Mace blew a stream of smoke, staring at the mesh-caged light in the ceiling.

The lawyer cleared his throat. 'Look, Jack my friend,' he began, 'I have not so much time with you, shall I tell you what I propose for the appeal?'

Mace looked down at him as if the sound had come as a surprise and he was seeing him for the first time. He stared unseeingly at his visitor, then blinked, his eyes clearing again. 'You do what you think best, Joe. First, I've got a job for you. I want you to give Miller an answer, personal like.'

Silverbach shook his head. He was getting out of his depth . . . if the Law Society should learn . . .

'You must not tell me anything, my friend, anything at all which could endanger our professional standing. I am your lawyer and I cannot . . .'

'Look, mate,' Mace cut in sharply, 'you don't earn your cut from me by sitting around on your backside and spouting law. When I want something done, you do it, otherwise I don't need you any more. Got it?'

Silverbach nodded cautiously. 'I only meant . . .'

'I know what you meant,' Mace said easily. 'Well,

forget it. There's a thousand in this for you if you do as you're told. Think about that instead.'

Silverbach clasped his hands tightly under the level of the table. 'What do you want me to do?' he asked quietly.

Mace leaned forward, speaking softly. 'You tell Miller that I'll need a breath of fresh air about half past eleven tomorrow night. E wing, E. 18—he'll know what you mean. Tell him it's a single cell and nothing's changed on the inside, they'll want to know that. You've got it straight?'

Silverbach repeated the message carefully. 'You're sure we weren't overheard?' he asked, glancing nervously at the door.

Mace laughed shortly. 'The screw's having a crafty fag down the corridor. I'm a good boy in here, remember?'

As Silverbach left the prison, he felt a cold dread sweep over him. One day, he reflected morbidly, they will not re-open the gates for me.

The spring sun squinted through the industrial haze which was already rising over the city, and Colin Harvey flicked down the visor above the windscreen to cut out the glare as he turned into Bridge Street and recognized Leric's car parked at the kerbside. He drew up behind, got out of the car and walked across the pavement towards his reflection in the plate-glass window of the motor showroom. Thee DI had left his home shortly after Leric's call, anxious to see for himself what the Sergeant had found at the garage. The padlock was hanging loose on the front door and Harvey went inside and caught Leric cat-napping in the office.

'Hallo, gaffer.' The Sergeant dropped his feet to the floor and rose from his chair, stretching. 'Have you been to the office yet?'

'No,' Harvey replied, glancing around, taking in the details, 'I thought I'd come straight here. Where is it?'

Leric took him into the workshop, explained how he had found the trolley and showed Harvey the adaptor and the gas-barrel lance.

Harvey picked it up carefully, using his handkerchief. 'What about prints?'

Leric shrugged. 'Might be, I haven't disturbed anything just in case, but I doubt they'd be that careless. They went to a lot of trouble to repaint the oxygen bottles, so I'd say they're too cute to have left their dabs about.'

Harvey examined the rest of the equipment, making a mental check against the details he had learned from the briefing at the Forensic Lab. 'It'll be interesting to see how that stub matches up with this,' he said finally, turning the adaptor over in his hand. 'No serial number, eh? They must have had it made to order.'

'Yes.' Leric yawned, tired after the stimulus of his discovery. 'Probably tailor-made for the job. I'd like to know who dreamed up the idea of using it on flesh and blood, he must be a right charmer.'

The DI replaced the tube on the workbench. 'I'll get a photographer up here before it's moved and then it'll be up to the lab to do their stuff with it—until we can put a hand to it, we're no further forward.'

Leric grinned. 'Why don't we put the whisper out that we're nearly home and dry, might loosen a few tongues?'

'Some of their local henchmen might change sides to save their own necks, you mean?'

'It's happened before, gaffer. If they think we're about to knock off the Londoners, they'd be falling over themselves to get 'em off their backs.'

'It might work. All we really need now is a tie up with Ted Spauling, the warehouse fire and this place. If we can get something definite from the lance and with Irene Spauling's identification to bolster it . . . Mind you, we'll have to tread light, though, these fingers are pretty sharp; if we jump before we're ready to make it stick, they'll walk out laughing, and French's squad'll want to know what the bloody hell we're playing at.'

Leric leaned on the bench. 'We've got a big stake in this business now, though—it's our knock-off by right, not some flash geezer down at the Yard.'

Harvey smiled. 'You don't think much of the Yard, do you, Leric?'

The Sergeant spat dry. 'All fancy chat and Savile Row suits, if you want my opinion. When this lot go down the stairs, it ought to be here, in this city, not at the Old Bailey.'

Harvey turned towards the door. 'I'll have a word with Strickland. Type up a full report of your findings here, it was a good bit of work, and one in the eye for your old guvnor, Harry Landon.'

Leric followed him out to the cars. 'That's what you get by sticking to the book, gaffer, a nice tidy search, but no results. The trouble with Landon's lads is they've got no imagination.'

Strickland called a conference as soon as the lance and other equipment from the garage was safely in the care of Anderson's experts. It was confined to the detectives of the inquiry team, now enlarged to more than a dozen experienced officers, including a sergeant and detective-policewoman from the squad's criminal intelligence section. They crowded into the Co-ordinator's office and waited for Strickland to start the session.

He sat hunched at his desk, tapping a pencil on the clean blotter-pad until they were all present. Leric closed the door and stood at the back of the room. Harvey sat beside Strickland in the chair reserved for the operations officer.

'Now then,' Strickland began, calling their attention, 'I don't think we need bother the city for this briefing.' There was general amusement; they had all heard the story of the fruitless search at the garage.

'Just to update the position,' Strickland went on, turning slightly to pull the cord of the extractor fan fitted into the window, 'Sergeant Leric has dug up one or two interesting items from Spauling's garage which should provide us with some useful lines of inquiry, and Inspector Harvey—' he waved the pencil to his right —'who has collated the whole investigation, has a witness, Spauling's wife, who identified the men Sand and Crouper as the two Londoners who called for her husband and took him away with them. I have just spoken to Commander French of the Number 9 squad, and he says there have been no significant developments from the London end, except that another man, named Brady, is believed to be up here with the other two. Very little is known about Brady, except that he is a confidant of Alex Shapiro's and has been seen with various known criminals who are considered to be among the hierarchy of Shapiro's orginazation in the East End. He has no known criminal record. Another significant point, this time from our end, is that although we have made considerable efforts to trace the movements of these men here and the locations they have been using, Spauling's garage has been the first real lead. Obviously, one or more of them stayed there at one time or another, but it's equally obvious that they must have alternative accommodation and have moved on since we raided the garage.'

Strickland leaned back and motioned to Harvey to take up the narrative.

'Bearing in mind that we had only a limited team operating at the outset of the inquiry,' said the DI, 'results were surprisingly poor because the usual sources of information had either been silenced or taken out of circulation. It looks now as if the Londoners have used underworld contacts, either by force, intimidation or persuasion, to keep out of sight, and they've done it so successfully that we have been unable to penetrate this cover. Now you all know the problems of working without even a whisper from the other side.' There were murmurs of assent. 'That's right,' Harvey went on, 'it's almost impossible in a conurbation the size and nature of this city. We wouldn't know where to start looking for these jokers, but—' he rapped the desk-top with his knuckles to emphasize the point—'one thing is certain : they are here and they are still operating. Without doubt, they are effecting a take-over of the underworld, a selective weeding-out of resistance and coercion of the rest. The motive?' He shrugged. 'I don't have to spell it out. These characters are professionals, they think professionally, operate professionally, and the reason behind their interest in this city obviously lies in the anxiety of our friend Shapiro to extend his empire outside London, where he is being subjected to some considerable pressure. We have good reason to believe, thanks to Sergeant Leric's discovery this morning, that they are also under-estimating us, and the longer we can keep them in that misguided frame of mind, the better. What we do need is some way of breaking down the silence of the local criminals. We need,' said Harvey pointedly, 'to convince them that we are in a position to put these characters away for a good long time and that it would be in their interests for the future, to help us to do it. What it boils down to is a big con act. If they don't bite, then you might mention casually that charges of conspiracy are being considered, and that their names have been mentioned. There's more than one way to skin a cat.'

Strickland took over again. 'Any questions?'

The crime intelligence sergeant asked mildly: 'Assuming we do locate them, what then?'

The Co-ordinator folded his arms. 'We'll watch 'em with the observation vehicles until they make a wrong move or we get enough to lift 'em.'

The detective nodded. It was all part of his job to lie on the hard floor of a panel van watching or photographing suspects through the disguised ports in the bodywork.

'By then,' added Harvey, 'we might have a few cards of our own to play.' He was thinking of Barney Farrow and the interlude at the mortuary. There was also a good possibility that the fingerprints found at the garage and the thermic lance might turn up something conclusive.

'All right,' said Strickland finally, 'that's the position. It's a changing one and it's moving in our direction

—don't let's lose the initiative. They'll be rattled if they find the lance is missing, and even more so when they realize the police are making a determined effort to find them. Threaten them, cajole them, con 'em rotten if need be, but let's start getting results.'

He rose, concluding the briefing, and there was a scraping of chairs as the officers stood and left the office, talking among themselves. Leric went back to his desk and took a sheaf of yellow crime reports from his drawer, reeled one into the typewriter and began to itemise his search of Spauling's garage for the inquiry log.

CHAPTER XVI

CROUPER PUT the phone down and scratched the thick mat of black hair in the open V of his sports shirt.

'Tomorrow night,' he said to Sand, who had been watching him throughout the telephone conversation, 'we'll be out of this dump. Shapiro's given us the green light on the Farrow deal.'

'Bit unlike the boss, isn't it?' asked the second Londoner suspiciously. 'He's never paid off a mug before—the boot used to be good enough.'

'He's getting a bit crafty, that's all,' replied Crouper with a low laugh. 'This way's clean and easy, and what's a few grand between friends? I wouldn't reckon much on Farrow's chances of spending it. Shapiro wasn't born yesterday. Give today, take back tomorrow, see what I mean?'

A nasty smile played on Sand's lips. 'Keep 'im sweet till we've got what we came for and then . . .' He sucked his teeth and drew a finger across his throat.

Crouper lit a cigarette and continued to scratch his chest. 'I wouldn't be surprised if Mr Farrow doesn't find himself in a bit of bother, only it won't be around here. He won't be able to run far enough, Shapiro's got him covered, and he'll get his gelt back, one way or the other.'

The Londoners had spent the day in the living-quarters above the betting shop, drinking and playing cards; waiting for Shapiro's instructions. The news that they were to agree to Farrow's terms had come as an anti-climax at first until Crouper explained the subtlety of the situation.

'Farrow's a hard knock, or he'd have cracked when he saw what was happening to his mates. It could take for ever to wear 'im down and we'd be stuck here until the local law found out the score, then we'd have to turn it in. Farrow could sit it out like a cat up a tree—he knows we won't croak him, not while he's got the key to the whole operation. This way, we sew it up and move out and leave Mr Farrow to someone else.' He kicked a piece of loose lino down with his foot. 'The operators will be here day after tomorrow, and by that time we'll be back down the East End.'

Sand crossed over to the telephone. 'I'd better give Lincoln a tinkle and see if anything's moving.'

'The only thing that's moving for him,' said Crouper with a coarse laugh, 'is his arse. I wouldn't trust that little fag any farther than I could spit a brick.'

Sand reached Lincoln at the You-Too and hung up after a brief conversation. He turned to Crouper with a worried frown. 'He says the law 'ave been there with a lot of fanny about how they're going to pinch us for the Spauling job. What do you think about that?'

'They haven't got a smell on us,' Crouper replied easily. 'Anyway, we'll be out of it by tomorrow.' Nevertheless, he felt a tightening in his stomach. 'It's just a come-on. If they'd got anything, we'd have had the heavy mob breathing down our necks before now. Once we're back in town, they can whistle.'

Brady, who had been sleeping in the flat above, was standing in the doorway in crumpled shirt and slacks. 'Come off it, mate,' he said harshly, 'if the law's taking an interest, they've had a buzz from French's mob in the Met. It's time we got out of it.'

'Look, fireman, this isn't my idea. I've just had a call from the boss, he wants this deal with Farrow sewn up. If you don't like it, and you wanted no more heavy stuff, phone him yourself.'

Sand shrugged. 'Do yourself a favour, Brady. We're safe enough here, nobody knows about this place, and at least this way we can kiss this town goodbye tomorrow night.'

'Be expensive,' said the toolman, eyeing his visitor with the inbred suspicion of his trade. 'Cost you five big ones, in advance.'

'I was told you were the best—expensive, but the best.'

The toolman watched him, face blank. 'Still interested, son?'

The visitor looked quickly around the crowded bar, the old stained woodwork, dirty cornices and cracked windowpanes; the cold, well-worn quarry tiles. The Eagle was a fraternity pub, a short distance but a world apart from the bright neon of the city centre. The occasional stranger who ventured after dark into the dirty back streets around where the Eagle stood, flanked by battered hoardings and bill-boards, left the neighbourhood without his wallet or teeth more often than not. A group of long-haired youths in leather jackets crowded round the bar, jostling each other, looking for trouble; a blowzy middle-aged woman, her hair frizzed from peroxide and lacquer, sat on a corner stool, face flushed, mouth slack, a glass of stout at her elbow. The toolman was still watching him, waiting.

'You were recommended.'

'Doesn't change the price.'

'All right, can we talk?'

Expressionless, the toolman half turned to the chrome and plastic juke-box he had been leaning against, and dropped a coin into the slot. He pressed the buttons without selecting the records and a pop tune began to thunder from the speaker, drowning out the babble of conversation in the saloon.

'Nobody'll hear a word over that din; now talk away.'

'The contract's a return trip, out and back in. Can you manage it?'

The toolman sipped his gin, a small wiry man in a light chalk-stripe suit, his thinning hair brushed across his head above a narrow angular face; watchful eyes. 'You were recommended right, son, what exactly were you told?'

'That you were on offer; that you could walk into the nick and get a bloke out, for the right price.'

'That's about right. What's your proposition?'

The second record dropped on to the turntable, heavy with drums and electric guitars. Behind the bar, a shirt-sleeved barman glanced up from the pint glasses he was washing in a cracked sink and scowled. They used to have a piano and some real music, a bit of a sing-song, not this pop rubbish . . . he hardly noticed the two men talking quietly near the record machine.

The toolman considered the contract carefully before committing himself. He was the best, no doubt about it. He'd got his nickname and reputation by proving there wasn't a lock made that he couldn't tickle. As a locksmith, he could have made an easy living, but he'd found calculated larceny an even more profitable outlet for his special skills. And the time he'd spent in prison, he'd turned to his own ends. The long hours tapping platinum points out of old telephone equipment in the prison workshop had given him plenty of opportunity to consider the locks inside the gaol, information which would put him on easy street once he was outside again. Quietly and discreetly, he had cased the locks, the double-action mortice for the interior grille doors; the single Chubb of the cells. He'd watched the prison routine closely, spending sleepless nights counting the footfalls of the night patrol punching the time-clocks on the galleries; he'd learned the strict order in which the clocks had to be operated, or else an alarm rang in the duty PO's office. The information had been gained piecemeal; from a trusty in the kitchen, for instance, the important fact that the night dog patrol in the prison grounds spent half an hour at a time drinking tea or napping in the warm kitchens. When he finally walked out of the prison gates, the toolman was satisfied that he would need no official invitation to go back inside again. Someone who wanted out badly enough would gladly pay big money for his very special knowledge.

The contract appealed to him—there was hardly any risk. The party wanted to be out of the prison for just an hour, and then put back in his cell as if nothing had happened. The reason was of no importance to the toolman. He didn't want to know. He could do the job, pick up £5,000 for a night's work and no one would be any the wiser. He'd taken the precaution of having the visitor checked out as soon as the first approach had been made, and the reports were satisfactory, but he was a cautious man, unwilling to take excessive risks. Only the punks chanced their arms, and he was too old for that sort of game. He was a professional, a specialist, and so he'd arranged the meeting to sound out the man for himself.

'Wants it away in a hurry, doesn't he, your mate? Doesn't give me much time to make the arrangements.'

'It's got to be tomorrow night. What's the problem?'

'I'll need a couple of drags, one for 'im and one for me.'

'That'll be arranged.'

'How about the pick-up to take 'im back? I'll be working to a tight schedule.'

'He'll do anything you say, just tell him where and when.'

The toolman nodded. 'I'll not want anyone else about queering up the pitch.'

'There won't be, you're on your own, we realize that.'

'The party inside, he's got his end sorted out, has he?'

'He'll be waiting for you. Do you need any gear or any help?'

The toolman looked up sharply. 'I'll get me own help, son. You won't know no more about it. Just cash on the nail as far as you're concerned. Leave the rest to me, understand?'

'Sorry, mate, I didn't want to—'

'Forget it, just remember to do the job my way, and if I find you've steered me wrong, I'll pack it right in, no messing.'

'Don't worry about that, the information's on the level. You'll want to know his name, though . . . so you'll recognize him.'

The toolman ducked his head again, finishing his drink and peering closely at the visitor. 'Never mind the monniker, the cell number's enough for me. I don't want to know who he is, only the mugs ask questions like that, and likely as not they just get trouble for askin'. I'll meet the contract, no more, no less. Now you sort out the cash, eh?'

The pubs were closed, small knots of men stood unsteadily at street corners in the pools of light thrown by the lamps, laughing and smoking a last cigarette, reluctant to make their way home; the strip light of a fish-and-chip shop attracted a few of the drinkers. A corner café, propping up a row of terraces in a dark side street, was shuttered with rusting wire mesh grilles, still strong enough to ward off the bricks and bottles of the vandals.

A knot of young Jamaicans, their faces gleaming like polished ebony, charged along the narrow footpath, arms linked, occasionally bumping into a passer-by, and a ragged vagrant in a threadbare overcoat stumped along the gutter, stooping now and again to pick up a cigarette end. The city was winding down for the night, a slow, agonizing process in the tough district around the city prison.

The green fifteen-hundredweight van which had been chosen for the job threaded its way through cross-city traffic, past the row of drab houses which stood sentry along the face of the prison wall; the homes of the warders, overshadowed by the black bulk of the gaol, paint flaking from the front doors which opened directly on to the pavement.

The van drew into the kerb beyond the turn of the wall, outside the double gates of a builder's yard on the other side of a canal which ran under the roadway. The toolman opened the door, dropped to the pavement and moved quickly over to the gates which were set back from the road. He had made a last guarded inspection of the padlock half an hour before and had selected the skeleton key which would open it. With one swift movement, he dropped the lock from its hasp and swung the gates open. The van turned in, lights off, and the driver parked beside two other vehicles, identical but for the builder's name on the side. It would pass a casual inspection.

The toolman closed the gates behind it, replaced the padlock and moved back to the pavement, walking towards the bridge which was flanked by a chest-high brick wall. The approaching traffic was thinning slightly now and he saw a police Panda slow down at the prison gates a hundred yards away and then accelerate past him. The toolman watched the car disappear up the road. It was the time to commit crime, he thought acidly, gauging his steps, alert for any undue activity on the pavements: the 11 p.m. change-over of the police shifts, when the coppers who had been on duty since three were anxious only to get back to the nick and book off, while their reliefs were none too keen to replace them on the emptying streets. Time for a couple of behind-the-bar bracers at a handy boozer, out of sight of the gaffers. Coppers were human, after all. The toolman watched the street, leaning on the bridge parapet. At the far end of the bridge, close to the gates of the builder's yard, stood an old Victorian urinal and the toolman retraced his steps to the green ironwork entrance set in a face of chipped stained tiles which had once been white but were now a dirty brown. He went inside, past the row of stalls, to the cubicles at the rear, dropped a penny into the slot of the shiny, worn brass lock, opened the door and slipped the hasp back into place. Standing on the lavatory seat, he could easily open the skylight and a shower of rust and dirt fell on his shoulders as he forced the narrow pane open and hauled himself up through the opening, cautiously finding his footing on the broken brickwork which abutted on to the blue brick wall of the aqueduct below. He glanced fleetingly down at the black water, feeling with his feet for the wide girder of the bridge support which ran below the roadway, slanting down to the towpath under the prison wall. His feet found the rivet heads and he moved carefully along the wide top of the girder, the road bridge looming above him and the light from the street-lamps falling behind him as he inched towards the narrow gravel path. He moved by instinct through the darkness to where the second man, who had already crossed the girder from the builder's yard, was waiting under the wall.

He had carried the equipment and the toolman ac-

L

cepted a black linen hood and pulled it over his head, arranging the slits for his eyes; a face could so easily be picked up in the swinging beam of a torch. They had worked together before and the toolman had selected his helper for his own special talents, the ability to climb like a cat. He was a screwsman by profession, and had mastered the art of scaling seemingly impossible sheer walls. He had one important task in the operation, the wall.

They crouched in the darkness, and the toolman watched the luminous second hand sweep the face of his wristwatch. The timing had to be perfect. He visualized what was happening inside the prison; the dog-handler who patrolled the grounds at night would be stopping at the kitchen door now, commanding silence from his Alsatian, as he slipped inside for a mug of hot sweet tea. He no longer allowed the dog to roam off its lead ever since the incident when he was attacked by his own animal in the pitch blackness. The Alsatian would be tied to a drainpipe by its choke chain. Only two others would be on duty inside the security wings; one of the principal officers on call and the night patrol man, walking the long galleries where the inmates had been locked in their cells since 8.30 p.m. All the interior gates were locked and the night patrol man had only the time-locks to concern himself with. The rest of the prison staff had left over two hours ago.

The toolman counted the seconds, then tapped the other man's shoulder. He moved away into the darkness and began to climb, feeling with fingertips and the toes of his canvas-topped yachting pumps for the cracks between the century-old granite blocks where the mortar had flaked away. It was a simple climb for a professional, spreadeagled close to the rough surface, patiently finding his footholds until he pulled himself on to the top of the wall, flat on his stomach, and unhooked a tubular stretcher with four long rubber grips from the harness across his shoulders. He fitted the frame into place, dropping the nylon scaling nets over both sides of the wall, and the toolman came up, taking a little longer and testing the net as he climbed. They descended hand over hand to the prison graveyard. The toolman crouched below the overhang of the wall, listening, but there was only the sound of his own breathing. The second man was a black shape beside him and together they strained their eyes to reorientate themselves with the already familiar surroundings. Satisfied, the toolman indicated that the operation should continue and the second man dropped to the ground, lying face down at the base of the wall where he would wait for the toolman to return with the party who was to go outside. They would be inside the prison for exactly four minutes.

The toolman skirted the exercise yard, past the corrugated iron side of one of the workshops, and took the last twenty yards to the cover of the security block at a crouching run. The five wings radiated from a central core, the well of the prison where the main staircases and security control point were, and the toolman moved silently along the wall until he came to the end of E block and ran his gloved hand over the plate lock of the solid exterior door leading out into the exercise yard, which was thrown open during the day to provide ventilation in the fetid, dank cell blocks.

He ran a finger over the face of the lock, familiarising himself with its contours, calculating swiftly. It was as he had expected and locks were his business. The toolman reached into the breast pocket of his windcheater, glancing up at the black face of the prison wing. The job would require his full concentration, working by touch alone. The Hobbs pick was delicately balanced in his hand, thumb and forefinger feeling the movement on the milled edge of the two florins, bored and brazed together to provide the manipulation of the fine steel tube which carried one of the skeleton wards of the picking device. He inserted it deftly into the lock, rotating until there was pressure from the mechanism. The miniature capstan was pressed into the palm of his hand and he leaned close to the door, straining for the tell-tale responses.

Gently, gently, he forced himself to breathe shallowly, anxious not to crowd his ears with extra noise inside the mask. There was always the terrible temptation to hold your breath, but he had learned to control his breathing, mouth open; to inhale and expel his breath silently. The tube carrying the second ward slid into the lock and the toolman let it find its own level, pressing gently on the four pins of the capstan until it was engaging with the lever gating inside the mechanism. He began to move the florin wheel, just a little more pressure, a fraction to the right. The bloody brass lever was binding, didn't the bleeders ever oil these things? Despite himself, he was sweating lightly and his nerves were beginning to jar. It was taking too long. He forced himself to be patient, if his concentration broke now . . . He moved the wheel again, feeling for the stump which would throw the gating once he could line them up properly. He swore softly. How the 'ell could the hamfisted bastard who fitted this call himself a locksmith? Come on, you swine, give. The lever moved

past the tight spot and the toolman's expert touch felt
the steel silver core of the pick find the face of the
gating, and with a finely balanced pressure on the capstan, he swung the wheel to free it and was rewarded
with the sharp click as the bolt sprang back into the
lock. The door was open.

He waited, crouched beside the door, checking his
surroundings. Silence. No bounding Alsatian to rip at
his arm and throat. No alarm bells. So far, so good. He
glanced at his watch, shielding the face with his free hand.
The night patrol man would be leaving B wing, yawning
probably, bored certainly, with only the sound of his
shuffling slippers and the animal noises of the sleeping
inmates for company. He had time.

The hinges were as bad as the lock, and the rust-
cramped spindle squeaked as he pulled on the door,
alarmingly loud in the silence. The toolman risked
opening the exterior door only wide enough for himself
to slip through. He stepped into the narrow space between the solid door and the interior grille and closed it
carefully, his back to the galleries. He turned and
looked down the long, familiar walkway between the
cells, illuminated by the harsh lamps set in the bare
brick walls which sent a grotesque spider-web of shadow
through the mattress-coil mesh strung between the iron
platforms running along the four galleries and rising to
the high roof of the wing. Every third light was burning
at night, sufficient for the patrol to see at a glance if
there was anything amiss. He would have to move
quickly. The open metal stairway to the landing was
at the far end of the block, but first there was the double-
action mortice of the grille gate, his next objective. It
was no match for the toolman's pick. He reset the

adjustable terminal steps, the light winking off the face of the florin wheel where the barrel of the pick pierced the Sovereign's profile. The grille opened easily and the toolman moved swiftly down the narrow corridor, past the identical doors of the cells, their flat faces broken only by the flaps of the Judas spy-holes through which the inmates could be checked as they slept. His rubber soles moved silently until he reached the foot of the stairway, E 18. Half-way along the second landing. The toolman moved up the stair, glancing down at the bottom gallery through the latticework metal steps which by day clanged and rattled from the footfalls of a hundred prison issue boots.

The night patrol would have reached the time-lock in C wing. He would pause until the exact moment, fit the key into the clock, turn it once and let it fall to his side again. He would be walking now, glancing occasionally into one of the cells, following his routine orders.

The toolman moved along the gallery counting the numbers printed on the cards in the narrow wooden holders on the wall beside each cell, scrawled occasionally with remarks and instructions for the warders. There were never any names. A green card carried the number 18 with the observation in blue Biro: Transfer for Appeal. He flipped open the Judas trap, then turned his attention to the lock. It was the easiest of all, for the Prison Commissioners in their wisdom had decided that the exterior doors should be the security strong-points of the gaol. Even if a man succeeded in getting out of his cell, he would be barred from escaping from the block. He drew back the single bolt and adjusted his pick with micrometer precision, manipulating the instrument with skill, and the door swung open.

The man inside was ready and waiting. Without a word, the toolman handed him a linen hood similar to the one he was wearing and relocked and bolted the cell door. By the time he had finished, the prisoner was masked, standing on the gallery in his stockinged feet. The toolman nodded approvingly; he was a careful one, this man whose name he didn't want to know and whose money was buying a few hours' freedom. He tapped the prisoner on the arm of his denim tunic and together they slipped back to the staircase, their long shadows chasing them along the dimpled metal catwalk and down to the ground floor.

The toolman motioned to his charge to wait while he relocked the inside gate, the pungent smell of confined humanity heavy in his nostrils. He closed the exterior door securely behind them and they crouched under the overhang of the cell block, listening to the night.

The night patrol man would be crossing the centre now, heading for D wing with nothing unusual to report. The silence was absolute. Where the 'ell's that damned dog? the toolman asked himself anxiously. Still tied up at the kitchens? Maybe, or else back on patrol inside the wall, ready to stumble on the fresh scent of intruders. Forget it. He pulled his fears up short. The dog patrols were a big joke, it was no time to panic.

They followed the same route back, two fleeting black shadows sprinting across the exercise yard to make their way finally to where the climber was waiting patiently under the wall. He helped the prisoner up the scrambling net and the toolman followed, suddenly overwhelmingly anxious to be far away from the prison. They waited on the towpath until the equipment was dismantled and then recrossed the girder, each holding the arms of the prisoner sandwiched between them to make sure of his footing on the narrow steel ledge. No one spoke until they reached the safety of the van.

'Nice touch, that,' said the prisoner, pulling off his mask. 'The patrol won't go near the graveyard after dark. You blokes have done your homework.'

The toolman grunted. The price didn't include idle conversation. 'There's some gear for you in the back of the van,' he said shortly. 'We've got a motor for you around the corner, so just keep your head down until we're in the clear. We'll be going back over the wall sharp on one-thirty—' he'd picked the time when the majority of the police patrols returned to their stations for their meal break—'and if you're so much as a minute late, it's off.'

The prisoner nodded in the darkness and climbed into the back of the van. 'Where shall we meet up later?'

'The all-night café on the ring road, there's always motors on the car park and one more won't be sussed. Drop your drag there and we'll have it picked up. It's straight, so there's nothing to worry about.'

The toolman closed the rear door of the van, twisting the handle shut, and after a whispered conversation with the driver, he went back to the canal and scaled the brickwork to the lavatory roof. The open skylight was as he had left it and he dropped down into the cubicle, completing the deception by pulling the chain before slipping the lock and stepping out on to the tiled floor. The place was empty and he went outside, glancing up and down the street. A couple, arm in arm, disappeared around the corner where the café stood opposite the prison gates, he would have to watch for them, but otherwise the street was deserted. It would only take a second.

He listened at the yard gates for the muffled sound of the van's engine and dropped the padlock, swinging the one gate open. The van reversed out and pulled into the kerb as the toolman replaced the lock, his eyes alert for any movement on the empty street. There was none. He got into the passenger seat of the van as the driver pulled away and turned to the prisoner who was leaning against the side in the back.

'If the screw takes it into his head to have a butcher's through the Judas, what'll he see?'

'Me in me bunk, pal, I've taken care of that. Stuffed some gear under the blanket. He won't suss a thing.'

The toolman nodded. 'It's my neck. Just wanted to make sure, that's all.'

CHAPTER XVII

BARNEY FARROW called on the caretaker in his quarters on the ground floor of the service flats. He rang the bell, flipping his cigarette-end out beyond the pool of light thrown from the entrance hall, and when he turned the man was standing in the doorway in his shirt-sleeves.

'Evenin', Mr Farrow,' said the caretaker, recognizing his visitor.

'Hallo, John.' Farrow leaned his hand against the sapele wall panel. 'Sorry to call so late, but I'd appreciate a favour.' He took a five-pound note out of his trouser pocket.

'Any time for you, Mr Farrow, you know that, any time at all,' said the caretaker. He hadn't missed the fiver.

'It's a bit delicate, John, you know how these things are, I don't want it to get around . . .'

'You can rely on me, Mr Farrow,' replied the caretaker with a confidential wink. 'What can I do for you?'

'There's a couple of blokes comin' to see me half past twelve, by arrangement, if you know what I mean. Bit of trouble over a bird and her old man's cutting up. I'll have to smooth 'im over, only he might turn nasty.'

The caretaker nodded knowingly. The tenants' private lives were none of his business, and a fiver was a fiver in anybody's language.

'I'm not bothered for meself, John,' Farrow was saying, 'only I don't want any trouble round here, so perhaps you could keep an eye out for them when they come up, and I'll give you a tinkle on the service phone if there's nothing to worry about. But if you don't hear anything after, say, ten minutes, perhaps you'd pop up to my place, just to be on the safe side.'

The caretaker looked interested. 'It'll be a pleasure, Mr Farrow. I know how it is, a bit of skirt's more trouble than it's worth. I remember this maid, when I was in the hotel business . . .' He pulled himself up short. It was no time for anecdotes. 'Anyway, that's all water under the bridge now. I'll come right up if I don't hear from you and make sure everything's all right. You never can tell with some of these characters, nice as pie one minute and then . . .' He waved a hand expressively. 'Would you fancy a plate of sandwiches, or a pot of coffee at the same time?'

'No, that's all right, John, I don't want to trouble

you any more.' Farrow pressed the note into the other man's hand. 'Have a drink on me, eh, and thanks for your help.'

The caretaker touched his forehead in a half salute. 'You can count on me, Mr Farrow, nothing's too much trouble for a gent like you.'

Farrow smiled with his mouth, and went back to the lift. In an hour's time it would be all over, and if Shapiro's boys tried to pull a fast one, they'd get more than they bargained for.

He let himself back into his flat and threw his jacket over a chair, crossing the soft carpet to the coffee table with the bottle of whisky on top. He poured half an inch into a glass; it seemed as if he had been living on the stuff ever since that bloody copper had pulled Spauling's body on him. Farrow sipped the drink, it would have to be only a small one, just enough to brace him for what he had to do when the Londoners arrived. It was the only chancy part of his plans. By tomorrow, he would be long gone, they would have to get up very early to catch Barney Farrow. Oh yes, he thought, they'll try. Only a mug would expect Alex Shapiro to part with fifty without a second thought. They'll come looking, of course, but they'll have to find me first. He stretched back in the chair, finished the drink and lit a cigarette. It was just a matter of waiting, and the waiting was beginning to make him feel edgy.

The car turned into the access road at the rear of the flats and began to cruise past the row of tenants' garages behind the block, the driver leaning forward slightly for a better view through the windscreen. He was no stranger to the area and the sight of a couple of open doors in the long line of garages confirmed his recollection that there were always a few of the apartments to let. He drove to the end and turned into one of the empty garages, cutting the engine and the lights, then got out of the car and pulled the up-and-over door down gently until the catch caught. There was no sense in taking the risk of leaving the car out in the open.

He walked softly along the footpath towards the rising bulk of the flats, picked out by the squares of light from curtained windows; past an ornamental wall with wrought-iron fixtures and across a landscaped lawn deep in shadow. The door to the fire stairs was where he remembered it and he pulled it open, staring into the blackness beyond and ignoring the time-switch light-button on the wall. He began to climb the concrete steps, feeling his way with a gloved hand on the metal balustrade, past the first landing and on up to the second floor. He opened the heavy fire-door and gave his eyes half a second to make the transition from almost total blackness to the dim glow inside the utility space; crossed the composition floor and glanced through the glass panel in the far door to satisfy himself that the landing was clear. It would be very soon now, he could feel the tension building up inside him, winding up like a mainspring, pulling his muscles taut. Out on to the landing, he kept his hands to his sides, walking quickly. There were four flats, flanking the twin lift shafts which ran up the centre of the block, the outside doors finished in a grained wood veneer, shining in the diffused light. A Chubb viewer had been fitted to the door since he was there last. He smiled and pressed the doorbell, listening to the muffled chimes deep inside the flat.

'Who's there?' said a man's voice.

It was unmistakable, flat and toneless. He waited quietly outside the door, watching the little thumbnail set in the woodwork. It opened suddenly.

'What the 'ell are you doing here?' Farrow stood in the doorway of his flat, silk shirt open at the neck, with the tie hanging loose, a surprised expression on the lean face. 'I thought . . .'

The visitor shrugged. 'Hallo, Barney boy, I heard tell you'd stand for the three-card trick if someone didn't put you right.' His voice was calm, controlled, almost with a hint of sadness.

Farrow moved backwards, stumbling against the wall, unable to stop a feeling of panic. 'You gave me a right turn.' The voice was verging on hysterics, as his mind groped for a solution.

The man stepped into the flat, closing the door firmly behind him.

The primal urge which had gripped him was beginning to ebb as he left the flats by the same dark exit and he was surprised to find the wide lawn bathed in pale moonlight. The sky had cleared and he breathed a lungful of the night air as his conscious mind took over again and began to check off a mental list of priorities.

The fat envelope which he had found in the inside pocket of Farrow's jacket was safely tucked under his windcheater, and he glanced down at it quickly to satisfy himself that the address he had automatically scrawled on the front was the correct one, then moved along the dark side of the block, avoiding the wash of the moon on the manicured expanse of grass. He made his way quickly back to the garages, pleased with his own caution. No snooping copper would have found the motor hidden here, he thought, sliding the door open. He got into the car, reversed it out on to the tarmac driveway, and rolled slowly towards the road. Once clear of the neighbourhood, he pulled in to the kerb beside a post-box and dropped the unstamped envelope through the slot; the recipient wouldn't object to paying the double postage. A heavy lorry roared past, the tarpaulin-covered load swaying, diesel fumes belching from its exhaust and the tailboard lights flitting between the dwindling concrete arches of the mercury-vapour lamps suspended above the wide carriageway. He looked at his watch, and then pulled open the door of the telephone kiosk beside the pillar-box.

Leric let the phone ring twice before he answered it. He had spent all night feeding the bull to cheap punks in countless dingy clubs and bars, and had collected just a handful of half-promises for his trouble. He glanced across the squad office to where Colin Harvey was hunched at his desk, leafing through the latest batch of reports from the teams of detectives now assigned to the inquiry. The DI stirred at the sound of the phone and Leric saw that his eyes were red-rimmed from the fatigue of long gruelling hours on the job. They had worked a straight eighteen, checking, re-checking, pushing the men who became careless as the hours of routine dragged by.

Leric picked up the 'phone. 'Yes, what is it now?' he began irritably, snatching a glance at the electric clock on the wall. It was twenty minutes past midnight. 'He's still here, hang on . . .' He held the 'phone at arm's length and called across the room. 'For you, gaffer . . .'

Harvey rose wearily, came across the room and took the phone from the Sergeant with a grimace. It hadn't stopped ringing all day.

'DI Harvey,' he said shortly, and recognized the voice of the duty inspector in the central information room. Harvey listened for a long minute. 'Just come in, eh?' He glanced at the clock. 'All right, we're on our way. Can you put out a city broadcast for the rest of my lads? And you'd better get Mr Landon out of bed if you want to keep your job.' He put the phone down and turned to Leric. 'We're in business, get your coat.'

Leric groaned. 'Not another one . . .'

'Not on your life.' The fatigue was slipping from Harvey's voice, 'it's the real thing this time, Leric, looks like Barney Farrow's finally come across. He's got our friends round at his flat.'

'The London team at his drum?' Leric echoed. 'He called to tell us that?'

'That's what the message says. "999" call to the information room just a few seconds ago, they passed it straight on.'

'He's going to turn 'em in, gaffer?'

'Looks like it. Put a snap into it.'

Leric slipped on his jacket. 'We'll need the full turn-out, and Landon's heavy mob as well.'

Harvey was out of the door, striding down the corridor towards the car-park stairway at the rear of the police station. 'We'll sort that out when we're on the road.'

They took the squad Westminster they had been using all day, and Leric set the tyres squealing as he accelerated out of the parking space. Under the dashboard, a monotone droned from the radio speaker : 'All mobiles of

the Regional Crime Squad proceed to Hamble Court,
East Rise, and await further instructions. Victor Tango
Control to all mobile units of the Regional Crime
Squad, proceed to Hamble Court . . .'

They walked with stiff-legged arrogance towards the
foyer of the flats, the collars of their light overcoats
turned up against the night air. Only Brady paused at
the rear door of the bronze Mark Ten in the parking
bay across the entrance drive to the block, his eyes
watchful for anything out of place, the slightest hint of
a double-cross, but the fancy low walling and slim mushroom lamp-posts looked innocent enough. Sand and
Crouper waited for him at the glazed double doors
under the ceramic awning.

'Let's get on with it,' Crouper said irritably, 'Farrow's
not going to take any chances, not while we've got the
bite on 'im. Besides—' he tapped his breast pocket—'it's
the cash he's interested in.'

Brady, annoyed suddenly at his own misgivings,
stepped between them and pushed open the door. It
looked as if Farrow had had enough, and the sooner they
were out of it the better. 'No sense in taking needless
risks, I was just checkin'.'

'He'll be all right,' Crouper replied as they waited
for the lift. 'He's seen the light at last. He knows if he
gives us any trouble, he won't have a prayer. Farrow's
got his head screwed on.'

They rode up to the second floor, unaware that their
arrival had been watched by the shirt-sleeved manager
from the unlit living-room of his ground-floor flat. He
stepped out into the lobby and watched the lift indicator

halt its ascent. 'A right handful,' he murmured to himself.

Crouper was reaching for the bell-push beside the door when he noticed it was ajar, and he grunted in surprise, pushing the door of the flat open with the palm of his hand. He turned to the others, 'What do you make of that, then?'

They could hear the sound of water drumming somewhere inside.

'Bit casual, isn't he?' began Sand, edging forward for a better view of the interior.

Brady realized that they were too far committed now to turn back. 'Go on in,' he said firmly, 'it sounds like he's taking a shower. We've dropped on him flat-footed.'

'He knew the time we were arrivin',' Crouper snapped, closing the door behind them and walking through to the living-room. The bathroom noise was louder now. He glanced around the flat, standing in the middle of the carpet. 'Not bad for a sucker.' Then, raising his voice: 'Hey, Farrow, come on out of there!'

Brady could feel the hairs on his neck beginning to prickle. Everything was wrong. The front door open, table lamps burning, an almost empty whisky bottle on the table. He moved quickly across the room, following the urgent sound of running water. It was the way he had felt wielding the lance inside the warehouse; when he had learned that Spauling was dead; an inner certainty of trouble. He jerked open the bathroom door and recoiled as a blast of steam burst from the room. He peered inside, eyes smarting as the hot vapour dispersed into the hallway, and saw Barney Farrow crumpled in the sunken rectangle at the foot of the shower, hair plastered to his skull; shirt and trousers clinging to his

M

body; knees pulled up under his chin and the exposed flesh lobster red under the boiling jet from the shower head. A wooden-handled kitchen knife was sticking out of his neck and a long river of blood ran down the front of his sodden steaming clothing into a swirling red whirlpool around the open plughole.

CHAPTER XVIII

COLIN HARVEY examined the terrain carefully, working out the operation step by step in his mind, unconsciously following the guidelines of the squad's standing orders for raiding premises. The flats were set on a triangular site, rising at the rear in a wide landscaped lawn bordered by low ornamental walls which helped to conceal a row of garages beside a rear tarmac drive, illuminated here and there by single-bulb electric lamps. A thin row of poplars veiled the rear aspect, the top branches sharp against the moonlit skyline. He had to take into account the many things which could happen within the space of a few seconds and plan to counter them, like a chess player working three moves in advance of his opponent.

Leric came round the edge of the flats, walking silently on the grass border. 'All set, gaffer,' he murmured, and pointed out the deployment of the four carloads of detectives surrounding the building.

'The dog van in position?' asked Harvey quietly as they stood together in the shadows.

'Over by the garages. Four handlers ready to go on the signal.'

Harvey took the blue plastic Pye two-way radio out of his mac pocket and raised the aerial; he spoke rapidly, his mouth close to the set. 'This is Harvey. Keep the channel clear and take your orders from me. We're going in now.'

He nodded to Leric and they walked back to the crime car where Veitch and McKenzie were waiting. Veitch stepped out of the car as they approached. 'Control say Mr Landon's on his way over with a couple of crews from the city squad. They've done a check on that Mark Ten with the Met. It's one of theirs all right.' He nodded at the bronze Jaguar standing parked in the bay opposite the entrance to the flats.

'No sense in letting Landon in on the knock-off, gaffer,' Leric began. 'We could wait all night for 'im to stick his size twelves in.'

Harvey ignored him. 'Who's on the fire-escape, Sergeant?' he asked sharply.

'Carter and the Number 6 crew,' Leric replied stiffly, trying to gauge the expression on the DI's face in the darkness. 'All experienced men,' he added tartly, anxious to get on with the job ahead.

Harvey looked up at the flats. Here and there a square window of light blazed out from the dark bulk; he couldn't be certain from the outside whether Farrow's flat was one of them. They would soon find out. He turned to the two DC's, Veitch beside the open car door and McKenzie sitting in the passenger seat. Two more detectives were leaning forward from the rear seat, their faces white smudges in the darkness.

'Get your pegs then, lads,' said Harvey. 'Let's get it over with.'

Six officers, including himself, he calculated swiftly. Should be enough. Any more on the inside and they'd be stepping over each other's toes; less, and they might come off worse in a scuffle. He gave the order to stand by on the radio, leading the way to the canopied porch of the flats.

Brady tore his eyes away from the crouching form in the shower recess and swung on Crouper, grabbing the lapels of his overcoat. 'You stupid bastard,' he spat viciously, 'we've been set up. Who else knew about this meeting?'

Crouper struggled to collect his wits, fear gnawing at him like a creeping paralysis. 'No one, I swear to God, fireman . . .'

Brady pushed him back and they stumbled into Sand, who was staring blindly at the body. 'He's bleedin' smilin',' he gabbled, his voice breaking, 'smilin' with a blade in his neck, like he's laughing at us.'

Brady hit him across the face with an open palm. 'Pull yourself together or we're done for. We've bin set up, I tell you. We've got to get out of here, and fast.'

Crouper hardly heard him. 'What about the stuff we came for? We can't face Shapiro without it.' He dragged himself free from Brady's grasp and began to pull drawers from the sideboard, scattering the contents on the floor.

'Forget it . . .' Brady began, but Crouper was on his knees now, heaving the padded cushions from the settee in his frantic search. Brady left him, moving quickly towards the door. It was time he thought for himself, and there was no time left . . . They'd walked into a trap, of that he was sure. If anyone could recognize a pro killing, he could, and this one bore all the hallmarks. The

stab wound to the side of the neck, finding the spinal
cord between the vertebrae; someone who knew Farrow, who had walked into the flat without arousing the
man's suspicions, for there was no sign of a struggle;
someone who could kill with one blow, and then the
real touch of the professional : the boiling shower
playing on the body to make it impossible to determine
the time of death. A pro job all right. He was icy
calm now, scheming quickly, a nerve twitching erratically
in his left eyelid. Forget Crouper scrambling about the
flat like a lunatic, he told himself; forget Sand, still
mesmerized by the sight in the bathroom. Get the hell out
of here and quick before the ceiling falls in. He ran to the
entrance hall and reached for the door handle.

The caretaker slipped on his official jacket with the
embroidered badge on the lapels, a determined expression settling on his face. Ten minutes he had given
it, and there'd been no call from Farrow. He was a
little ashamed of himself for the trepidation with which
he had watched the minutes tick by on the mantelshelf
clock, willing the phone to ring. The last thing he
wanted was to get involved in something unpleasant, but
on the other hand, there was the fiver and he had
promised. He was tugging an arm into the jacket
sleeve when the door buzzer startled him.

The foyer seemed full of hard-faced men and the
two nearest to the door were staring down at him. One of
them held something up in his hand, and the caretaker's washed-out blue eyes flickered with bewilderment.

'Police,' said Leric, showing his warrant card, Harvey
standing at his shoulder. 'You'll be the caretaker,' began
the DI, watching the surprised expression on the

man's face. 'There's nothing for you to worry about, but we need the master key to Flat 6.'

'Flat 6,' echoed the caretaker stupidly, his eyes swivelling. 'What's going on?'

'Nothing to worry yourself about,' Harvey reassured him again, 'just routine, that's all.'

'But that's Mr Farrow's flat, I was just on my way up there.'

Leric raised an eyebrow. 'Got visitors, has he?'

The caretaker nodded. 'Three blokes went up a few minutes ago. Mr Farrow's a respectable gentleman, he just asked me to go up and see everything was all right.'

'We'll take care of that,' said Harvey. 'Now, if you'll let us have the key . . .'

The caretaker blinked. 'Yes, certainly. I didn't want to get involved, only I did promise . . .'

Harvey took the key from his hand. 'You've been a big help. Stay inside until we come down, we'll have a chat then.' He turned to the waiting D's. 'All right, lads, let's get moving. Two of you on the lifts and the rest follow me.' He turned to the stairs, taking the composition flights three at a time, with Leric and the other four detectives close behind. They crossed the landing and Harvey located the flat, deploying his men with quick movements of his hand. 'Right.' Leric nodded when they were in position, covering the stairhead, lift gates and flanking the polished door. Harvey turned the key swiftly in the lock as Leric, McKenzie and Veitch stood waiting, ready to rush inside. He pushed the door open and caught Brady a heavy blow on the shoulder.

'Get him,' Harvey barked, but the fireman was too quick for them. He lashed out with a foot, catching Veitch in the groin, and as the detective went down,

Brady sent him sprawling backwards and snatched his chance to reach the fire-escape, disappearing through the far door before they could reach him.

Leric and the other two were inside and Harvey spoke quickly into the radio. 'One on the fire-escape.'

Leric saw Crouper turn from the chest of drawers in the bedroom and grab the base of a table-lamp, ripping the flex from the socket. He threw himself at the man's knees, knocked him off balance and they rolled across the carpet, crashing into the bed and grappling for an advantage. Leric felt a wave of sickening pain sweep over him as a blow caught him in the stomach and he tugged a handful of hair, pulling the man's head back until he could press the face into the carpet. Christ, he's a big bastard, it's got to be quick or not at all, thought Leric, straining with all his strength to keep the man down. Suddenly, the struggling stopped and he saw McKenzie kneeling on Crouper's back, his fingers clamped on the pressure point in the man's neck. He snapped the handcuffs on to the limp wrists and dug the other detective in the ribs. 'All right, son, let the bastard breathe again.' Crouper's face was livid, and blood trickled from a split lip to form a pink froth at the corner of his mouth.

'Coppers,' he spat disgustedly, 'dirty coppers.'

Leric brushed off his clothes and moved into the lounge where three officers were manhandling Sand out of the doorway, kicking and writhing between them. He found Harvey in the bathroom, looking down at the body in the shower.

'No wonder they had a knock,' he commented as Harvey turned off the blast of water. 'With this lot down to them, every villain in the city will be marking their cards. We won't have any trouble with evidence now, gaffer, they'll be falling over themselves.'

Harvey crouched down beside the crumpled figure, noting the knife-handle sticking out of the man's neck. 'He must have tried to pull something on them. He knew he'd got it coming, so he called us first.' The DI tried to fit in the details. 'You'd better get on to the coroner's office, Leric, and get a photographer up here. We'll make this stick, all right.'

'What happened to the third one, Brady?'

Harvey looked up. 'Dog got him before he could reach the car, but he's put a couple of Carter's lads in the hospital.'

A shadow fell across the doorway and they turned to find Landon leaning against the door jamb. 'Sorry I missed the fun, lads,' said the city superintendent lightly, rubbing his hands. He nodded at the body. 'Friend of yours, wasn't he, Inspector?'

Harvey's expression didn't change. 'I don't know about friend, sir. He was either a fool or an informer, either way he was too late.'

They took the Londoners in to the central police-station in separate squad cars, each man handcuffed and flanked by detectives. Leric squeezed into the back of one of the grey Westminsters, sandwiching Brady between himself and one of the DC's, a heavy-shouldered young man with the build of a rugby forward. The Sergeant nodded to the driver and the small convoy moved off for the short drive to headquarters, where facilities were being prepared for detention and interrogation under the direction of Strickland, who had been roused from his bed on his own orders.

'Take a long look,' said Leric, nodding at the passing suburbia, 'that's the last sight you'll get of the outside for quite a while.'

Brady said nothing. He sat in silence, hunched forward by virtue of the fact that his wrists were manacled behind his back, his stockinged feet wedged under the front seat in an effort to make his position as comfortable as possible.

Leric wriggled in the cramped seat and took a packet of cigarettes out of his pocket. 'Smoke?'

Brady shrugged, and Leric lit the cigarette and held it to his lips. 'No sense in making it any more unpleasant than it has to be,' murmured the detective, watching the glowing tip of the cigarette as the Londoner inhaled. He glanced across at the other DC, who was staring resolutely out of the window. 'They call you the fireman, don't they, Brady?'

The Londoner breathed out the smoke, and said nothing.

'Not very talkative for a man who's got no form,' observed Leric quietly. 'I might be able to help you a bit, you know. Bloke like you, no previous, I might be able to put in a word back at headquarters, perhaps a lesser charge, accessory before maybe, if you're sensible about it.'

Brady turned his head slowly. 'You mean if I cough it and drop the others,' he muttered.

'There's no sense in making life difficult for yourself, is there?' Leric went on, flannelling the other. He gave the Londoner another pull on the cigarette and waited for the man to exhale. 'You could tell us what happened at the flat, for a start-off, why Farrow got croaked, that sort of thing.'

Brady watched the street-lamps flash by as the car sped along the deserted streets. 'What if I said he was dead when we got there?'

'Oh no,' Leric replied, shaking his head, 'pull the other one. You'll have to do better than that, how about it?'

'Son,' said Brady with a sudden harsh laugh, 'you make me sick. All you coppers make me throw up and as far as I'm concerned, you can all get stuffed.'

Leric stiffened. 'All right, Brady, make it tough, then. There's one or two things we'll be wanting to put you through the hoop on, like thermic lances . . . fireman.'

He waited for Brady's retort, but the Londoner held his tongue. Leric nudged him sharply with his elbow. 'And if you think Alex Shapiro's going to pull you out of this one by your bootlaces, forget it. We've got you on the hook, Brady, make no mistake about that.'

The Londoner eased his aching wrists. 'I don't know what you're talking about, copper. You must be mistaking me for someone else.'

'You're nicked, Brady,' snapped Leric, 'nicked straight up. By the time you come out, you'll be drawing your pension.'

'I'll tell you one thing,' Brady replied, wrinkling his nose, 'your strong silent mate here smells like the inside of a Turkish wrestler's underpants. Do you mind if we have the window open?'

The DC glowered across the dark interior of the car, his heavy face alive with anger. 'I'm not going to take that . . .'

Leric chuckled. 'Don't let him rile you, lad, he won't be so cocky tomorrow morning in the dock.' He glanced out of the side window as the car arrived at the police-station, and a score of detectives and uniformed men came out from the parade room to help transfer the prisoners to the cells.

Colin Harvey pushed the niggling doubt to the back of his mind and listened respectfully as Landon ran through the list of jobs which had to be done before they could leave the flat and seal it off with a uniformed man on guard until the morning.

He had sent Veitch downstairs to take a statement from the caretaker, and the photographer and scene of crime crew from headquarters had already arrived with the night man from the coroner's office. The case was already moving out of his hands through the official processes of handing over to the city force, for the crime had taken place on their territory and was theirs by undeniable right. The active role of the Regional Squad was more or less over.

'Well, Inspector,' Landon was saying, 'you can leave this end with us now, don't you think?' He paused to direct a group of officers conducting the detailed search.

Harvey nodded and left the city Superintendent in the lounge, carefully skirting the polythene bags containing the labelled exhibits for the lab. The body was still where they had found it in the bathroom, and he stood in the doorway blinking in the harsh light from the arc lamps which had been set up for the actuality pictures. A couple of shirt-sleeved detectives were crouched on the tiled floor working over the scene of crime notes, measuring distances and noting them in their books. He looked down at Barney Farrow, and felt a cold shiver at the sight of the bloodless lips parted in a seemingly mocking grimace. The knife-blade, he could see now, had pierced the man's neck almost exactly in the centre of the puckered scar which had earned him his nickname. The doubt came back, stronger now.

Why, Harvey asked himself, searching for a reasonable solution, had Farrow left it too late to save himself. And why, came the second question tumbling over the first, had it been a '999' call when Harvey had told him to ring direct? There was only one rational conclusion, he told himself, and that was that Farrow had not made the call at all. But then, who was it? Someone who knew of the arrangement with the Londoners, who would have benefited by what had happened; and that left the second conclusion, that the same hand which had held the telephone had plunged the knife into Farrow's neck. There was no evidence of a struggle, no skin traces under the fingernails, no slash marks on the hands or arms to indicate an attempt to ward off the knife attack. Had Farrow known his killer, trusted him even?

Harvey felt suddenly cold and tired. Did it matter, he reasoned finally. The Londoners had killed before this night, not enough evidence for a jury maybe, but sufficient to convince him that they were ruthless and without compunction when it came to death. And here, suddenly, was a case laid out for the police. Circumstantial, certainly, but damning all the same, and by the very perversity of their nature, he was confident that once the details became public, there would be no shortage of underworld information on the rest of the Londoner's activities.

Harvey turned on his heel and walked out of the flat, his limbs heavy from fatigue. It was, he supposed, the sort of rough justice to be expected of the city, a composite grey like the streets and the buildings, and far removed from the black and white of the law books. The mob was crushed and that was all that mattered. Justice, he perceived, crossing the courtyard of the flats which was now crowded with police vehicles, was a malleable commodity which could be squeezed and pummelled like putty into the cracks and crevices of the tight-laced rules of society, for which it had been fashioned.

He got into his car and started the engine, pushing the thought aside. There was still work to be done.

CHAPTER XIX

The day began, as did every day in the city prison, with the clatter of the warders' boots on the old iron galleries, and the metallic noises as keys jangled on their rings and were fitted into the cell doors at 8.30 a.m. unlocking. Cell doors were thrown open and the prison dragged itself from sleep, the inmates shuffling to the recesses to empty the foul sanitary buckets of another night's confinement.

In the remand wing, Jack Mace sat on the edge of his rusty iron cot, hands hanging limply between his knees, and waited for the screw to arrive. He looked up at the rasp of the key in the lock.

'Let's be havin' you, Mace,' said the screw, throwing back the door and poking his head around the opening. He was one of the middle-aged officers, given to doing the odd favour for an inmate if the price was right.

'Got the paper 'ave you then, Mr Jones?' asked Mace, reaching for a Rizla from his breast pocket. Newspapers were one of the few privileges allowed in the prison, and the warder handed Mace a copy of the local morning paper.

'See a mate of yours got done last night, eh, it was on the radio earlier,' he began, as Mace scanned the front page, drawing a deep lungful of smoke from the pin-thin snout he had rolled between his fingers.

GANGLAND KILLING, said the headline, and below in slightly less bold type, LONDON TERROR GANG CRUSHED IN POLICE SWOOP.

Mace shook his head and spat a strand of tobacco. 'Makes you glad for once you're safe in the nick.' He laughed and turned to the racing page.